DECEPTIONS

THE ROAD TO POWER

A NOVEL

JOHN PASCAL

JOHN PASCAL BOOKS

DECEPTIONS, a novel: 2023

Copyright 2023 by Pascal John Imperato
ISBN: 979-8-218-12838-8

Unless otherwise noted, Bible quotations are from the "New King James Version, Spirit-Filled Life" Bible. Thomas Nelson, publisher, 2018.

ACKNOWLEGEMENTS

The author expresses gratitude for editing by Rebecca Farnbach, leader of the Temecula Critique group, and by proof readers: Sarah Imperato and Alan Toyne. The cover painting is the original work of Doreen Terryberry.

This is a work of fiction. Any resemblance to real persons is purely coincidental. Well, except for Eve whose hand is on the apple and Satan playing the part of the snake.

DEATH AND LIFE

Be strong and of good courage for...the Lord

Your God will not leave nor forsake you. Dt 31:6

Paramedic Owen Wilson called to the driver from the back of the van. "Couldn't hear all of that. Where are we headed?"

The ambulance driver flipped on the siren. "Unplanned Mother Clinic—the nurse said it was urgent."

"Shoot, I'm supposed to be off duty--guess I'll take a cab home after. That clinic really needs someone with hospital privileges. Did they say what was going on?"

"A patient who's bleeding, but they want us to come around the back and turn off the siren when we're close."

A woman was jumping up and down and waving at them when their ambulance pulled up to the loading dock. The four men hustled out the gurney and their supplies. The woman called out, "You might be too late. Follow me."

They rushed into an upstairs room where a woman in coveralls was finishing up mopping the floor. She wheeled her pail out of the way and held up her hand. "Cuidado! Floor wet."

A still form lay alone on the treatment table partly covered with a sheet. A pale white forehead protruded from one

3

end, a long trail of auburn hair dangling off the edge beside it. Next to a bloody umbilical cord, her hand with delicate, long fingers hung down below the sheet--pink fingernails decorated with tiny white dots.

The first paramedic felt for a pulse, another readied a breathing apparatus and Owen placed cardiac paddles on her chest. No pulse. A few breaths were forced in, and Owen hollered "Clear!"

Her body convulsed, but there was still no pulse. They repeated the moves several times—no response. The lead paramedic turned to the nurse. "Sorry. We'll take her to the hospital to have her 'pronounced'. Your doctor's not available? Any relatives here? We'll need some ID."

The nurse had secreted herself into the corner of the room. She was shaking her head, hand over her mouth. Wide, searching eyes peered over the hand. "Doctor's not here now," she croaked. She went to a side counter and retrieved a tan cloth bag. It had embroidered butterflies and dog faces on it. Jingly things tinkled as she handed it to them. "Ann's purse—should have ID inside."

The men moved the body to their gurney and covered it completely. With the purse on top, they wheeled toward the door. "Thanks, nurse."

Owen accompanied them as far as the back door, and took out his phone to call for a ride. The nurse grabbed his sleeve. "Please don't go yet." Tears were streaming down her cheeks. "It's not just Ann. There's another patient."

Owen pointed outside to the paramedic van. "Should I bring them back?"

She shook her head. "No, just you."

"Really. Why just me?'

"Cause I saw you pray up there."

Despite the moment, Owen smiled weakly. "All right, please tell me your name and what's going on here."

She cleared her throat and wiped her cheek with her sleeve. "Sorry. I'm Celia Holt and I'm just a nursing assistant. I decided to quit today, so I don't care if I get in trouble." She motioned for him to follow. "Better just see for yourself."

Back up on the floor where they had been, another girl in a white uniform called to them. "Cece, is it all clear?"

"Oh, sure. You can take the patients to the exam rooms now."

Celia led Owen back to the same room. He gave her a puzzled look. "There's no one here."

"Yeah, there is." She opened a door to a supply closet and walked in. "Come on."

"You're making me nervous, Celia. Are you the patient?"

"No—well, I might need counseling, but that's not the point. Honest, I'm not playing a game. There's a patient in here."

Tentatively, Owen entered--gasped. There on a roll cart lay a blue-gray newborn infant covered with streaks of blood, gasping and gurgling. "Damn." Instinctively he picked up the infant and held it upside down. He cleared its mouth with a finger causing fluid to come out, and gave it a slap on the bottom. There was another gasp, then a cry.

Celia jumped up and down. "Yes, yes, yes!"

Owen cradled the infant in his arms. "What the h-e-double hockey sticks is a baby doing in *here*? Get me a towel or something, huh?"

Celia quickly produced a small blanket from a shelf and helped wrap the child. Owen smiled at the now pink face. "It's a girl."

"Oh, thank you so, *so* much. I was going to try this myself, but I don't know much about babies. They leave anything born alive here to sit until it dies. Then they put it in the freezer and sell it for body parts."

"Yuck." Owen's expression twisted in disgust. "But this girl is full term. What happens if your boss comes in?"

"Not good, right? I'm hoping we could put Ann's kid in your medicine bag. Maybe you could take her to a hospital or something."

6

Owen held the infant against him. She was now quiet, but gave him a little kick. He kissed the top of her head noting it had a large gash, and handed her to Celia. "I'm in."

He emptied out his treatment bag on the roll cart. She went to a shelf and brought him a large plastic bag. He filled it with his equipment and spread open his treatment bag.

Celia gently placed the infant inside and said, "I put my cell phone number in here, too. Please call me and let me know if the baby made it." She gave an excited little hop. "Come on. I know a back way we can get you out."

SURPRIZE

Whoever receives one little child like this in
My name receives Me.   Mat. 18: 5

Owen backed in through his apartment door with his arms full, calling out, "Honey, I'm ba…"

"Woah, are you *late*! Isaiah ate already and your dinner's getting cold."

"Sorry—should-a called, but wait 'til you see why."

Beth hustled out of the kitchen tying up some stray black hairs that had fallen out of her bun. She gave him a quick cheek kiss as he put two bags down on the coffee table. "Sorry, that was harsh, but I didn't know where you were. Got an extra call, did you?"

"Two calls. I think I better explain. We were headed back to the station when…"

A cry came out of his work bag. Beth's face exploded with surprise and she quickly spread it open. "Owen, my *God!* Whose is it?"

"Mother's deceased. They were going to let her baby die, so I snuck her out of the clinic."

Beth gently lifted the crying infant out of the bag and held her against her chest as she began rocking. "*No one* does that, do they?" She peeked under the towel. "A girl, and she's streaked with blood. Got a gash on her arm. and scalp. She was just born?"

"About two hours ago, and I still have to tie off that umbilical cord remnant and treat the lacerations. Tomorrow, I'll find out about her next of kin at the hospital."

The infant was quiet again and Beth sat on the couch. "Hand me that pen and pad you always carry." He complied and she began writing. "Here's a list of what we'll need right away from the drug store. Meanwhile, I'll get this poor little girl cleaned up."

PROBLEMS

The Wilson household was calmer the next morning despite being awakened so many times in the night with crying. Owen left early for work after his wife assured him not to worry. Twelve-year-old Isaiah was fascinated by the new arrival, but reluctant to hold her. He was puzzled by his mother making him swear to secrecy about the child, but he liked the idea of having secrets.

When there was a break between calls, Owen went to a private place and reached out to Celia. "Hi. The baby's doing fine—already putting down some formula. Tell me about her mother."

"Ann was so sweet. She said she was twenty—but I think mid-teens. She shared a room with some woman and worked as a waitress. She also said she got knocked up by a one-timer in a bar--said the guys' name was Sonny—not his real name, I'm sure."

"Did you know her well?"

"Not really, but we talked some. The last thing I remember about her was in the waiting room. A girl was sitting with her head down on her arms crying. Ann, near term herself,

10

got down on her knees in front of her." Celia's voice became strained. "She had her head against the girls and was stroking her back and quietly singing to her. The girl walked out of the clinic with a smile on her face and didn't keep her appointment." Big breath. "Anyways, Ann was coming in for checkups and prenatal pills. She told me once she was gonna keep her kid."

"Well, what went wrong?"

"Every time she came in, the clinic tried to get her to have an abortion—told her it would ruin her life to have a kid. I was supposed to say that, too. Don't know if they did anything about her complaints of spotting, but they told her there wouldn't be any complications. Every time they told her, 'The sooner the better.' Basically, they deceived her."

"Yeah, but she went to term,"

"I got her to make an appointment with an outside doctor, and she was just in our clinic to get her lab test results when the labor pains started. Our clinic nurse said she was in no condition to travel. 'Sign here,' she told Ann. 'We'll take care of it for you'."

"I haven't seen the autopsy but obviously there were complications."

"Yuh think? It was a breach—I couldn't watch. The placenta was in the way and blood was everywhere. They gave her shots--they said for pain. The doctor kept swearing. They

11

didn't have any blood for transfusions and—I guess you know the rest."

"Yeah, they don't have all the equipment needed and an operating room for cesarian section. They should have called for our ambulance right then. I'll bet the Medical Board and Health Department will be coming down hard."

"Not from what I've seen in the past. That clinic has big time political protection—seems women's health won't survive without it. Any other ideas?"

"Prayer."

"Roger that. Thanks for helping."

"Glad to, but Celia, you just saved a girls' life. God bless you."

#   #   #

When Owen returned home that afternoon, he found his wife holding the infant in a newly acquired padded rocking chair with a look of profound peace on her face.

He put his work bag down by the front door, came over and enjoyed a lip kiss. "I've got lots of information on mother Ann from Social Services. They have to notify the next of kin, you know, and apparently the only one living is a single uncle in Denver recently released from drug rehab."

Beth didn't say anything but nodded for him to go on. He said, "I gave the update I promised to Celia. She quit her job, by the way, but told me the father was a one-timer at some bar—never saw Ann again."

"So, this child is an orphan, and a hungry one, I might add." Do you have a plan?"

"Sure. I found out there are two state adoption agencies who would take an infant, but I didn't tell anyone I had one."

"Any Christian ones?"

"No, they're currently in litigation about a new law requiring them to offer placement to same sex couples."

"That's just awful. I hope they win their suit." The infant began to gurgle and squirm. "Honey, could you bring me the bottle in the warmer. It's on the kitchen counter."

The infant's 'pre-cry' mode quieted as soon as the bottle was delivered. Beth patted the seat arm of the chair next to her. "Owen, I just *know* this is a mission God has given us. Don't you think our little girl deserves a name?"

He chuckled. "And I'm sure you've thought of one."

Beth shifted the baby into a different position while she held the bottle. "I'm thinking, if you agree, of course, she should be named Zoe Ann. Zoe means life, and Ann is her mother."

"Perfect, that's beautiful."

"Good. Owen, darling, did you know that infants can talk with their eyes?"

"That's a new one on me. Uh, what did she say?"

"She asked me if I was her mother."

Owen released a nervous chuckle. "Now, don't worry. We'll find a good family for her, I'm sure."

Beth grasped his forearm and leveled a deep, penetrating look that flowed into Owen's soul. "I said, yes."

DECISIONS

Owen found his son, Isaiah, in the kitchen walking around the center island reading a book and munching on a cookie. "Don't eat so much. You'll get so fat the girls won't notice you."

Isaiah lowered the book and bestowed a patronizing look. "Teenage metabolism is higher than yours, Dad."

Owen chuckled. "Okay, genius, you won't be thirteen until next month. Look, we need to have a family conference."

"Sure, but I havta study up for the American History contest Monday. It's sponsored by a Christian University and I'm one of four finalists."

"Great, but this won't take long." He motioned for him to head for the living room. "Could you win a prize?"

"Oh, yeah." Isaiah grabbed another cookie, sprinted to the next room and plumped into an easy chair. "First prize gets all expenses paid for our spring field trip to Washington."

"Cool. That saves me money. All right, then," He pointed his finger. "Who wrote the Federalist Papers?"

"John Jay, Alexander Hamilton and James Madison."

"Good. Who won the battle of Brooklyn Heights?"

"Neither. The British claimed victory, but a miraculous

15

storm and fog bogged them down, so Washington's troops escaped their trap, and later they won the war, of course."

"Wooo!" Dad grinned. "I think you're ready. If I'm free, I'll come and watch."

Mother came out of the bedroom, gently closed the door and put a finger on her lips. "Not so loud, guys. Zoe Ann should sleep for a while." She sat on the couch next to her husband. "This is our family pow wow, huh?"

"Yes, and this is serious." He pointed at each one. "All of us should be in agreement, so let's bring Isaiah up to speed. Mother has gone into full Mama Bear mode over our new arrival. I'm doubtful about it, but she has a plan to keep the baby." He gestured to her. "Beth, you explain it."

She smiled at her son. "I think you know, we have tried to have a second child, but it hasn't happened. Zoe Ann has no real family, no papers and adoption would be a problem. Dad will explain more. Anyway, I'm thinking about going to my mothers for a couple of weeks, crash diet, and tell everyone I gave birth."

Isaiah threw his head back, looked at the ceiling and said, "Woah!"

"Okay, okay." Owen opened his hands. "Here is how I feel. If Christian adoption centers were open, I'd place the baby there, but I'd still try to adopt her. I read the centers are on full lockdown until the court settles the adoption by same-sex-couples thing. I don't want to hand her over to the county and maybe lose out on adopting her."

Isaiah shook his head. "Is this another test question? Christian charities have a First Amendment right to freely express their religious beliefs."

"Ah, but the government claims the moral high ground and insists on complete control."

"A total deception, Dad. So they'd close my Christian academy because it offends people who don't believe in God?"

"I wouldn't be surprised if they did." Shaking his head, "but, what your mother proposes is a deception, too."

"I see that, but *they* started the war, Dad. In a battle, particularly a just one, a general might fake to one side and attack the other. Is that deception wrong?"

Dad shook his head in thought but Beth responded in a gentle voice. "So, Izzy, you agree with my idea?"

"He raised a fist. "Full on! She's my little sister, now."

Owen laughed. "Okay, so we're the rebel crew, but we'll have to sneak the baby out so no one will see—and this is a strict family secret, agreed?"

Isaiah's' face became suddenly grim. "Uh, oh, I just thought of a serious flaw in our plan."

Concerned looks leveled in his direction. He turned to his mother. "Dad can't cook."

ANN

In his full-dress paramedic uniform Owen dropped by the Social Services office at the hospital. He hoped the stethoscope draped over his neck would add to the desired look of authority as he stood in front of a woman typing at her desk. "Ahem, Miss?"

After a few more pecks at her keyboard, she looked up, unimpressed. "Uh, can I help you?"

"Yes, Owen Wilson, AMT services. I brought in the deceased woman, Ann—uh don't remember her last name."

"Ann Smith—died in delivery?"

"Right, that's her. Thank you for your work in searching for the next of kin."

"That's our job. Too bad there is only an uncle in a rehab facility. He wasn't interested in arranging a funeral. He was only willing to take the twenty-seven dollars on her person and the money due her from Brews and Burgers where she worked."

"So, they weren't close."

She chuckled. "He only knew his sister had a kid but didn't know her name. Why are you interested?"

"Oh, not in him," He adjusted his jacket and bestowed a broad smile. "My wife knows someone at the restaurant and thinks she might want her personal effects."

The woman gave Owen a hard stare and brushed a lock of brown hair to one side. "Well, we have to keep records of all paperwork in her files for a period of time—drivers' license, bill from that so called clinic where she died—county regulations you know."

"What do you do with the other things—things of no value?"

"Charity if there's anything salable, but there was nothing worthwhile in her purse." She went to a shelf, pulled out a box and looked inside. "Good, we made copies of the papers already. We'd throw all this out in thirty days anyway, so why don't you just take it?"

Owen walked out with a plastic bag containing Ann's jingly purse. Before he drove off, he closed his eyes, leaned his head on the steering wheel and said out loud, "Dear Lord please forgive my lie about who my wife knows."

#   #   #

Owen strode up to the welcome counter at Burger and Brews with brusque determination. A tall, dark-haired girl turned to him. "Just one? Counter or table?"

"Neither. I'm with AMT Services investigating the Ann Smith death. Who here knew her best?"

The girl grabbed her blouse at the neck line and shook her head. "OMG we *all* knew Ann. Can't believe she's gone. They said it was from childbirth, right?"

"At the Abortion Center, yes."

"Really? Ann said she had finally decided to keep her baby—said she'd work something out."

"Uh, huh." He took out a notepad, trying to look detached and official. "Everyone here was okay with that?"

She crooked her finger so he would bend closer. She whispered. "Yeah, but not the boss. He told Ann, 'Lose the kid or lose your job.' Maybe she decided on abortion after all."

"So, she had one. Do you know her roommate?"

"Carla? Sure, she'd pick her up sometimes."

"Yes, Carla. We have her address, but would you know her last name by any chance?"

"Morales. She'd come here with a boyfriend sometimes."

Writing, "All right. Thank you. I think that's all."

The girl held up a hand to a waiting customer but asked, "But, she didn't hafta die, did she? What happened?"

"Besides a clinic's incompetence and greed? I'd say deception."

#   #   #

Owen sat in his car and mulled over his progress. *Beth wanted me to gather as much as I could from Ann to share with her daughter later. Must be more where she was living. I'm sure her death could have been prevented.* He put the purse on his lap and began a search. *Mostly cosmetics, a hair brush and clipped coupons. We could run a DNA on those hairs. Wallet just has her license and a credit card. Woah.*

He just noticed a zippered side pocket with her cell phone inside. *Bet they never noticed this.* Finding the battery dead, he plugged it into his car charger and was able to start it up and scroll the contacts. *There she is—Carla.*

Calling her number on his own cell, he was surprised that she answered promptly. "Carla Morales?

"Speaking."

I'm with the AMT Services investigation team following up on the death of your roommate, Ann Smith. Would it be all right if I came by and asked you a few questions?"

"Sure. I'm going out in an hour, though. Could you come over right now?"

Surprised again, Owen tried not to show it in his voice. "Certainly, Ma'am. Be right over."

It was not until he replaced Ann's cell in its pocket that he discovered surprise number three—a small notebook. It contained some names and addresses, a sketch of a dog's face and the new hours for Burgers and Brews. On the back page, she had written, "placenta previa—blocking cervix—Doctor Roberts recommends immediate C section if bleeding gets worse."

21

Flipping to the address page he found that Doctor Roberts was at County Hospital. She wrote next to his name, "April 26th, or ER if bleeding more." *Dang it. Why did she go to that other clinic instead?*

#   #   #

Carla answered the door with her hair half way made up. "Sorry for the way I look, but I want to know why Ann died."

He shook her hand. "Miss Morales, I'm Owen Wilson, EMT tech. Our preliminary analysis is she went back to the abortion clinic instead of following Doctor Roberts advice. Do you think she had decided not to keep the baby?"

Carla waved him inside and resumed working on her hair. "Nope. She was gonna have it. I think she went back for her lab work is all. It's crazy. She could have had it mailed."

Owen shook his head. "Too bad. Uh, the only next of kin we found was an uncle. He's entitled to get any personal effects."

"That's one more than I knew about." She gestured for him to follow. "This was her room. There's not much here some uncle would want. I'll give what's left to charity, but I guess you could take anything for him you want. I've got a new roomy coming on Monday—look, I've got to finish getting ready."

Owen stood alone in the little room. A wave of sorrow filled him as he looked around. On her bedside table was a book

22

called, "What Every New Mother Should Know." He couldn't bear to touch it.

Ann's only possessions seemed to be in the closet where an assortment of women's clothing hung—same for the little dresser—wait, there was a small pink blanket with a teddy bear on it. *Guess everything can go to charity.* Nothing seemed to be of real value but then, Owen discovered a jeans jacket with sewn-on decorative patches and hand embroidery.

Finally, he searched the closet shelf. It held pairs of shoes and an artist's sketch book. That was the real find—page after page of talented pencil drawings. Owen was about to head back to the living room but spun around. *Wait, that blanket—it belongs to Zoe Ann.*

Carla popped out of her room. "Look, gotta sprint, now." She held up an envelope. "Almost forgot. This just came for her." Looking at the armful Owen was holding, "Glad you found something for the uncle."

"Thanks. You can give the rest away. One last thing. We have her age as twenty on her license."

Carla laughed. "That's a fake. She was about sixteen, I think. I still can't believe AAA believed her claim and sold her driver's insurance. Ann did learn to drive, though."

"I guessed as much. Thanks, Carla. Call me if you have any questions."

Back at his car, Owen put the stash on the seat and looked at the letter. It was from the Automobile Association and addressed to the "Estate of Ann Smith."

He shrugged his shoulders and mumbled, "Guess there's no harm in my opening this." The letter read: "We have received a copy of the death certificate of Ann Smith from Oswego County. This notice is sent to the address of record as a check of authenticity before payment of the death benefit to Riverside Christian Fellowship. If our information is correct, there is no need to respond."

Owen leaned back in the seat. *Huh—didn't see that one coming.*

PASTOR VISIT

It was Saturday afternoon when Owen returned home. Isaiah sat on the couch, Pepsi in hand, feet on the coffee table. The closing credits for Star Trek scrolled on the TV. "Hey, Son, I'm back."

He flipped off the screen, retracted his feet and waved. "Hi, Dad. Seven of Nine is just so *hot*!"

Owen chuckled and put Ann's purse down. "No argument there. Could you bring in the stuff on my car seat?"

They laid out the items on the dining room table. Owen said, "All this belongs to your new sister, but she won't appreciate them until she's grown up. I learned a lot about her mother today."

Isaiah picked up Ann's phone. "Like being a smart penny-pincher? This phone service is only fifteen dollars a month and someone gave her their old 3G phone. Trouble is, it'll go dead in a few months."

"Her contact list was helpful. I made an appointment with her pastor at five o' clock and I'd like you to come."

"I—uh..." He crossed his eyes. "I've got hamburgers defrosting—could I pass?"

Owen grasped his shoulder and smiled. "I know you're still working on God's reality, Son, but this is a family matter. Ann left her life insurance to this church so we should meet her pastor. Also, we can hit a steak house after that."

"Well, since you put it that way."

#   #   #

Pastor Frank Lyndell ushered them into his counseling room. "I'm really crushed to hear about Ann's death. She didn't come to service every week but was a regular in our Women's Bible Study." He gestured for them to sit. "I'd like to know more about how she died."

After his description, Frank shook his head. "I'm crushed to learn she was going to *that* clinic. I know she was repentant and embarrassed about her pregnancy, but I wish she would have asked one of us for advice."

Owen's face squinched, giving Pastor a hard stare. "May I tell you something in strict confidence?"

"If you're not describing a crime, absolutely."

"We don't *think* it's a crime, but her child was left to die after it was born. A nurse assistant helped me rescue it."

Lyndell's head jerked back. " Wow! Is the child still alive?"

"Alive and well. See, we want to adop…"

Pastor stood up and raised his arms. "Oh. Praise the Lord! God *bless* you."

Owen stood up as well. "We heard the state cut off Christian adoptions, but we thought maybe we—my wife and I—could pretend it is ours."

"Oh, no need to try that. The state only cut off their referrals to us, not our license. I'm on the board of a local service. Where is the child now?"

Isaiah said, "In my mom's arms. She growls if you get too close."

Pastor Frank laughed. "A boy or girl?"

"A girl. We named her Zoe Ann. She's got big brown eyes that look right at you."

"Oh." He rapped on his chest and grinned. "And I gather you want to adopt her?"

Owen nodded. "You bet. We just didn't think it was possible."

"Of *course*, it is, and we'll facilitate it for you. We'll just need mother's birth certificate and a certification of live birth for Zoe Ann signed by a medical professional. Her birth certificate will follow. Oh, I don't suppose the doctor at that clinic would sign it."

"No, he doesn't even know she's alive, but I know a nurse who would certify it."

"Perfect! I don't see any problem, then. Did you know that Ann named our church as beneficiary?"

"Right--I guess because she had no family."

"We are her church family, but even though she never knew you, you're her family, too, of course."

"We feel like we are, and I really appreciate your helping with the adoption."

Isaiah's face brightened. "Say, that means we don't have to lie about anything, and Mom can come back."

Owen pointed a thumb at his son. with a grin. "I think he's tired of my cooking." Turning to Pastor, "I know your church will put the money to good use."

Frank raised a finger. "About that—I'll have to go through the Board of course, but my feeling is we should establish a trust fund for Zoe Ann. I'm sure Ann would have changed the beneficiary to her daughter had she lived."

At that, Owen's offered a hand shake but it became a hug with a blessing. "Thanks so, *so* much, Pastor. This is just wonderful."

Isaiah chuckled. "Yeah, I get my mom back and we still get to go to the steak house."

# # #

When they got to the car, Owen's phone was ringing—Beth calling. Before he could say anything, she spoke rapidly. "Sweetheart, I can't live with this deception. Mother agrees. We have to offer Zoe Ann for adoption and pray real hard that God gives her to us. You *know* how much I want her, but…"

"Beth, guess…"

"No, I know you guys do too, but it's just the right…"

"But, Beth…"

"Look, I know it would be awful if..."

He raised his voice. "Hey! We *got her*, darling! We will be her adoptive parents!"

Silence. "What? You went to an agency? We weren't going to tell anyone, Owen."

"I found out she had a pastor. I only told him in confidence and he assures me we're almost certain to be approved by the agency he works with."

"My gosh, that's *wonderful*. Okay, you're forgiven. Come and pick us up, okay?"

"On my way, Dear."

ENCOUNTERS

Five years have passed. Isaiah is completing his senior year at a Christian academy. Zoe Ann has taken her family through the terrible threes and the frantic fours and is in kindergarten. We find Owen washing the Paramedic Van outside AMT services on a balmy spring day.

His friend and co-worker, George, is lean, athletic and black. While Owen scrubs the roof with a foamy sponge, he mans the hose and polishes the wheels. He calls up, "I'm betting our grumpy, old Captain names you the new Crew Chief this afternoon."

"Really? Susan's been here almost as long as I have, and I think she's memorized every rule in the book."

"I know, and Roger got a medal for that heroic save last year, but he's new and you're the most respected senior. Besides, you served as acting Chief a couple of times. I'm sure he's asking you into the office for the promotion."

"Maybe, but don't forget Gretel. She agrees with his radical ideology and laughs at his jokes."

George laughed. "Yeah, a whole year of eyelash batting."

"Okay, hose off the hood." Owen tossed his sponge into a bucket. "Well, I sure could use the extra pay. My son will be starting college next year."

George splashed the hood, turned off the hose and tossed Owen a towel. "Cool. My oldest is still two years away. Where's yours going?"

"We don't know yet. He's got a scholarship, but the Christian universities he wants would be expensive even with a student loan."

For a minute the two toweled away before George added, "I hear you, and I'm not sure about college for my kid. Personally, I hope he'll be an electrician like his grandfather—pays real good, too."

They tossed their towels into a bin inside the garage and admired their work. Owen gestured toward the van. "There, sparkles like new."

George nodded with a pout. "Just wait. I bet the next call we get will take us into the mud."

"You remember that—a real mess, wasn't it? Okay, I better get upstairs and see what the boss wants."

#   #   #

Owen found Captain Fehrenbach reading a newspaper, leaning back in his desk chair, feet up on the desk. Despite the open window, cigar smoke filled the room. "Uh, you wanted to see me, Captain?"

He lowered the paper slowly, folded it, and pulled his feet off the desk. Fehrenbach was portly, well past his earlier days of ambulance riding, but with his slicked down black hair, he still looked youthful thanks to Bigen coloring dye. Dark eyebrows lowered as he put his cigar on an ash tray. "Wilson, when I say, around three o'clock, I think you should know by now I mean *promptly*."

"Sorry, Sir. It's ten after, isn't it?"

"There's been a complaint about you, Wilson."

Owen clenched his teeth and thought, *Uh oh, I hope that clinic isn't suing.* "Sorry to hear that. What's the problem?"

The captain wasn't offering him a seat. "Tell me about that weekly meeting you organized a month ago."

"Our prayer meeting? We invited you to attend, remember? We start at shift change so two crews can attend and almost everyone does. We think it's important to dedicate our service to God and ask protec…"

"Stop! You never asked me if you *could* do it. We receive government funds so you can't establish religious services. Also, you never realized how offensive that is to some who work here."

"But, Sir, it is entirely voluntary and we're not trying to establish anything. Would you prefer if we held it outside on the back patio?"

"No, not on our grounds. It's over, Wilson—but one more thing." He picked up his cigar and took a few puffs and took a moment to think. "The State is cutting back on our funds, so if we're going to replace the older van, you and a few others will have to go to part time—three days a week."

Owen stood open mouthed. "I, I can't make it on…"

"Oh, and everyone is probably wondering. I just promoted Greta Merkel to be your new crew chief. She has shown good leadership qualities in her short time here. Be sure and congratulate her."

NEW PLANS

When Owen got back to the apartment, he called his family to the living room and pulled a chair around to face the couch. Beth and Isaiah shared puzzled looks while daddy's little five-year-old climbed into his lap and snuggled her auburn curls against his chest. "Got some bad news, guys."

Isaiah volunteered, "Gonna work extra shifts?"

"Don't I wish. No, they cut me back to three days a week and, of course, I didn't get that promotion to Crew Chief."

"What?" Beth shook her head. "That's so *wrong*. You're the best man on their force."

Owen sent her an air kiss. "You might be a little prejudiced, but it could be Fehrenbach was really annoyed about my not asking permission for the weekly prayer sessions I set up. He's pretty woke, you know."

"Pfffh."

"Bottom line is we have to take a hard look at our financial plans, particularly Isaiah's college."

Beth said, "I'm sure they'd let me go to full time at Happy Maids."

34

"And I might be able to do some handyman work on off days, but all that still won't cut it."

Zoe Ann looked up at her daddy. "My piggybank is almost full."

Owen kissed the top of her head. "That's sweet of you, Darlin, but we'll figure something out."

Isaiah said flatly, "Don't worry. Time for me to confess. I really want to forget college and take that county job cleaning sewers." Smartass got a laugh.

"Okay, here's what I'm thinking." Owen pointed at his son. "Rather than the Christian university, we'll make it if—maybe just for the first year—you start at the State university. Meanwhile, computer-wiz, George, located an ambulance service hiring paramedics nearby the state university and it's only a hundred miles from here—a suburb of Chicago."

"Phoo." Beth squinched her face. "I'm not real fond of big cities. We'd have to move, and that's expensive, too."

"Thought of that. Our only car is on its last tires, so I'll trade it in for a used SUV that can pull us and a U-Haul."

Isaiah said, "Yeah, Mom, Dad and I can carry all the furniture we have." He gave Zoe Ann a stern look. "Course, we'll have to leave the spoiled princess behind in a work house."

From her perch on Daddy, Zoe Ann returned a stuck-out tongue.

Owen continued. "If I get the job, we'd leave in two months—just in time for Izzy to start in the fall. Meanwhile, I've begun working on getting a Physician Assistant certificate and now, working part time, I'll have more time to push it."

Zoe Ann hopped off dad's lap and, with puppy dog eyes, she looked up. "Can Snuggles and Bugsy come with us?"

"Of course—all your fuzzy friends."

Isaiah countered. "I don't know, Zo, Bugsy's ear has chocolate stains and Snuggles gets car sick."

Beth chuckled and pointed a finger at him. "Time to give it a rest, Izzy."

ORIENTATION

Isaiah Wilson left his college orientation feeling confused. His Christian high school had not prepared him socially for the state university. Activists were everywhere. Signs demanding freedom from student loans competed with BLM and rainbow banners.

Later, he'd be taking the bus from their new apartment on most days, but today he got to drive their "new" ten-year-old Chevy SUV. After all, it was his first day.

Isaiah smiled and nodded as he passed students shouting to free someone in jail. Returning to the student parking lot he was relieved to find it apparently peaceful. The only gathering was a group sitting on a low wall. His car was easy to spot since it was larger than the others, but especially easy today because it was covered with white foam graffiti and all the tires were flat.

He stood back aways, fighting off waves of depression and anger. The biggest words were, "fossil fuel pig." The vandals were meticulous. Even the "John 3: 16" bumper sticker was covered with the "Co-exist" one. He sighed. *Well, at least the good news is, dad has a tire pump in the back and it looks like they used shaving crème for their messages.*

Isaiah tossed his backpack in the rear seat and began to work on filling the tires. The students on the wall hoped down and stood behind him calling out taunts. He ignored them until he finished with the last tire. One threw something at him, ricocheting off the back of his head and landing next to him. *Hmm, looks like an orange peel.*

He got in, rolled down the window and called to his tormentors, "Thanks for the nice college welcome, guys."

One hollered back. "No f------ polluters allowed on campus, white guy."

Isaiah started the engine, began to back up and called out the window. "Hey, virtue flashers, this was our moving van. Think you know where to buy an electric truck?"

#   #   #

After a stop at the do-it-yourself car wash, Isaiah pulled into the parking garage below their new apartment and took the elevator up to their floor. His mother greeted him with a cheerful, "Hi, Izzy, how was orientation? Tell me about the classes you'll be taking."

"Sure. If I can have a couple of your chocolate chip cookies and milk, I'll try for the PG-13 version."

"Uh, oh."

He settled in at the kitchen table, devoured one cookie and pushed the rest to one side with a frown. Beth studied his face. "You're upset, Izzy. What happened?"

"For openers, let's jus say this sure isn't a Christian college. I want to be a History major—maybe even teach it one day. At the college we couldn't afford, they had courses like "America and Religious Freedom," "The Revolution that Shook the World," and "We Hold These Truths—The Constitution.""

"I take it, they weren't offered."

"There was one with American Revolution in the title and I signed up for that. There's dozens of courses in the History Department--one on Western Civilization. The rest are divided between Social Justice, black slavery and Marxist themes."

"Yuck. But there must have been other courses too."

The cookies looked appealing once more and Isaiah dipped one in the milk. "Sure. There are required freshman courses in Math and English—oh, but you can't use that word. They're called "First Year Courses" now."

Beth sat back in her chair and relaxed. "There, see? It's not all bad. I know you can cope with it. Meet any classmates?"

"Yup, and they decorated our fossil fuel nemesis, but I cleaned that up." He chuckled. "I can hardly wait for the second year, though. I get to take The History of Gender."

KINDERGARTEN

Most mothers took their kids to school on the first day of kindergarten, but the kids were expected to take the bus home. At noon, Beth stood with other anxious mothers at the drop off point. One asked her. "How do they expect the children to remember their stop? My Wes could get off anywhere."

"They get assigned numbers for the driver to announce. This is stop number six."

"Oh, I missed that, but knowing Wes, he could get off at sixth street."

"Now, Meg," Beth chuckled. "That's why we're here. They all know what their mothers look like."

Finally, "big yellow" arrived with flashing lights. Kids of all ages poured out. "I still don't see—Wes!" Meg ran to him and smothered him with hugs, much to his embarrassment."

Beth stood waiting by herself. The doors were still open and the driver was talking to someone. Zoe Ann appeared by the door playing a game that involved hopping down on each step.

Beth took her hand and apologized to the driver. Her daughter continued to hop along in the street and up onto the curb. Mother laughed. "So how was your first day at school?"

"Rribbit."

"Could I have Zoe Ann back, please?"

She looked up at her mother with wide, serious eyes. "Can't you tell I'm a bull frog now."

"I can see that, but we better teach Miss Froggy to walk 'cause we have almost two blocks to go."

"Froggies can walk, too."

"Oh, good." (But, they do take a skip every few steps.)

Back at the apartment after lunch, Zoe Ann took out the artwork she created in class. It depicted her family—not the usual stick figures, but recognizable people standing side by side. Beth tapped the drawing. "You might not realize it, dear, but your art is really precocious. This is from your mother, you know."

"Pre—what?"

"It means you have early artistic talent. Anything else going on at school?"

"Teacher gave each of us a test."

"Really? But, she hasn't taught you anything yet. What kind of test?"

"A private test—in a room with some other lady. She asked questions and wrote down what we said."

"Interesting. Can you remember any questions?"

"She said it wasn't for parents to know."

Beth forced the look of horror off her face. "Okay, I'll keep it a secret."

"Promise?"

"I promise. What questions."

"She asked about things we like to do, and stuff."

"Maybe your teachers want to know you better."

Zoe Ann went quiet for a moment and stared out the window. "Mommy."

"Yes?"

"Mommy, do you think I'm really a boy?"

"No, silly, you're a girl, of course."

"The lady said because I like to play ball, the color blue and science, I might really be a boy inside."

Beth was grinding her teeth but forced a calm voice. "Some things both boys and girls like. Hey, I know what."

Large expectant eyes turned up to her. "What, Mommy?"

"I've got the champion game of the Women's National Softball Team recorded on the DVR. Wanna see the last few minutes when they were tied 4-4? It was really exciting."

Big grin. "Okay, Mom."

They settled in on the couch with Zoe Ann snuggled up against her mother. "Keep your eyes on these fantastic plays by our champion women. They are the girls in the *blue* uniforms."

AMERICAN HISTORY

Those who control the present control the past.

George Orwell

Isaiah bravely sat in the first row while the professor made his introductory remarks about the course outline covering America from settlement to mid-1800's. Professor Schmidt was a tall, slender man wearing sandals and an oversized Navajo pattern shirt. His full red beard had not been trimmed in a while.

Schmidt displayed a pained grin. "I'm sure you all realize that the first colonists to America brutally displaced the peaceful residents from their native land. With their overwhelming guns, the white man settled in, enjoying his conquest. Even today, the American Indian remains marginalized and separated."

Isaiah sat quietly shaking his head as the professor continued. "The conquerors thought the forests would make productive farmland and they would profit by selling crops to Europe. So, thousands of beautiful trees were chopped to the ground." The class knew it was time to groan in protest.

"The United States was founded as a 'slaveocracy' in 1619. Indigent African people were forced into slavery. I have summaries of the Pulitzer Prize winning 1619 Project for each of you and copies of the book are available in our library."

The professor picked up a book from his desk and began to strut back and forth in front of them. "You'll find that the image of America taught to your parents was designed to glorify the conquerors and needs to be corrected. For instance, one of the first laws made it a crime to free a slave."

Isaiah was surprised to see his own hand shoot up. The professor scowled, but said, "Yes?"

"Sir, who captured those African men, sent them here and wrote the early colonial laws concerning them?"

Behind the round metal rims, Schmidt's eyes narrowed. "The point is, those white settlers made windfall profits on the backs of slaves by selling their cotton, rice and tobacco. They made no attempt to change the slave laws."

"But, if they wanted to, *could* they have changed the laws their English king wrote for the colonies?"

The professor brushed him off with an arm wave and strode off in another direction. "Immaterial. See me after class."

"Bad laws and taxes, Sir. Mary Grabar wrote a book debunking the 1619 Project and with no representation, it was worth fighting a revolution for freedom, don't you think?"

Schmidt spun around and snapped, "Slavery persisted for a *century* past that. Don't interrupt. We'll get to that later."

GOOD NEWS

Owen opened his apartment door, loosened the top button on his uniform and called out, "Honey, I'm back. What is that heavenly smell?"

Beth hastened out to meet him with a kiss. "It's just some meat I'm browning for the stew. How was your first day at work?"

"Better than I expected, dear. This EMT group is twice as big as my former one so I thought there'd be even more rules, but they're a friendly bunch. Captain Barnes welcomed me personally and said his office is always open for complaints and suggestions."

"Thanks, I needed use some good news." Beth grinned. "Time for a coffee break. Get comfy. I want to hear more before Zoe Ann gets back from school."

By the time Owen had pulled off his boots, put up a leg on the coffee table and settled into the couch cushions, his wife came in with the steaming brews. "Hey, thanks, Hon. Guess what? My new Crew Chief—name's Sam Jackson, said it was his tradition to get to know all new hires. He would like us to have lunch at his place Saturday."

Beth sat on one side of the couch and curled her knees up so she could face him. "That's great—so there's a whole new atmosphere at this place, huh?"

"Oh, yeah—men, women, and every race. It's kinda like a family atmosphere. Sam's black, by the way."

"I'm so relieved, but now that you're back to full time, maybe you should wait awhile before suggesting they have prayer meetings, huh?"

Owen grinned and put his coffee cup down. "Won't have to, Beth. They have one before every shift starts."

"What?" She giggled. "But won't someone complain?"

"Nope. They meet in a gazebo in a public park next to the property. I think everyone shows up."

"You just made my day—oh say, it's almost time to meet your daughter's school bus. Wanna come?"

#   #   #

Zoe Ann came down the school bus steps, her face full of concentration. With a large piece of cardboard under each arm, she jumped off, flapping wildly. Dad caught her as she fell forward toward the pavement. "Woah, little angel. I think that needs more practice."

She looked up at her parents with a pout. "If birds can do it, I can too."

Beth took her cardboard "wings" and they headed down

48

the sidewalk. "God gave birds special bodies that can fly. Besides insects, they're the only ones who can, darling."

Zoe Ann had clearly given this much thought. "Angels can fly too, Mommy."

Owen snort-laughed. "She's got you there, Hon."

His daughter took his hand and looked up at her mother with a "there, see" expression. Owen chuckled. "I tried that too when I was eight or nine. A buddy of mine helped me make a pair of three-foot wings out of balsa wood. Our plan was to glide off a high place and maybe glide half a mile."

Her expression, now bright with excitement, "Did you fly, daddy?"

"Well, yes and no." He chuckled. "I did glide about fifteen feet from the tool shed, but I hit a tree and sprained my wrist. It turns out that wings are more complicated than they look."

Beth's turn for the "there, see" look.

Owen countered. "But, someone did invent hang gliders. When we get home, I'll show you what they're like on the computer."

Beth slapped her forehead. "Oy."

Back in the apartment, and after the hang gliders, Zoe Ann asked if she could go down to 4B and play with her best friend, Gini. "We're making up a new game called 'oppressor'."

Startled, mother asked, "Woah, what?"

"Oppressor. They showed us a video in school today. If you're white, you are an oppressor of the poor, and if you're black you are oppressed."

"Good grief. What do you think that means?"

Zoe Ann shrugged. "Not sure. I told Gini it means I can tell her what to do, but she says it means I have to give her free stuff."

Beth had to smile. "Okay, I'll take you down to the Adams apartment, but we'll talk about that video before bedtime."

On returning she found Owen reading in his reclining chair. With a sigh, Beth said, "Honey, parenting is getting harder."

"I heard all about that oppressor stuff. School board meeting is a week from Tuesday. Do you still have that megaphone from cheerleading?"

AFTER CLASS

When History class was over and the students began moving toward the exits, Schmidt motioned for Isaiah to follow him into an antechamber. He sat down behind at a small desk and leaned back in an office chair. With a grin and a tilt of his head, he said, "Well, Wilson, you certainly are outspoken."

Isaiah eased off his backpack, put it on a straight chair and leveled a calm gaze on his professor.

"This being the first day of class, I'm inclined toward leniency. Where did you go to high school, Wilson?"

"Covenant Academy, Springfield, Sir."

Schmidt chuckled, pulled out a bottle of spring water from a drawer and took a swig. "Parochial school, of course. I'll bet they taught you that God founded this country, right?"

"No, Sir, but we were founded by God-fearing men who followed biblical principles to write our cons…"

"Oh, stop. I see we have a lot of deprogramming to do. Long before the Revolution we were founded by slave traders and this core of white supremacy persists today."

Isaiah persisted. "The United Nations states that in the world today, there are still fifty million in slavery." Schmidt scowled.

Isaiah stood silently. He noticed that the water bottle had a yellow tinge. Schmidt nodded and offered a thin smile. "All right, here is what we'll do. Rather than interrupt the flow, I'll announce that all questions will be written and handed in when class is over. I'm sure we'll eventually get the truth into you. Any more questions?"

"Yes, Sir, I understand. I'll be submitting my questions to you in writing, but may I ask one now?"

Schmidt gave a hand-toss go ahead.

"Will you be answering them?"

YUCH

The school bus came late and the mothers could hear the driver shouting something as he pulled up. When the doors opened, the children were somber, plodding down the steps with deliberation—even Zoe Ann. Beth put her arm around her child's shoulders. "What's going on, Darling? It's Friday. Kids are supposed to be happy."

Zoe Ann didn't answer but kept up with deliberate steps alongside her mother. A tearful Gini and her mom quick-stepped past them without speaking. Beth stopped for a moment, hands on hips. "Okay, 'Missy,' spill it. Why was the driver angry?"

"Lotta bad kids is all."

"Fighting?"

"No, the older boys were touching the younger girls, but they didn't get me."

"Oh, that's awful, Darling. No wonder the driver was angry. Their parents need to know."

They reached the elevator in their apartment. "Aren't you going to push the buttons?" Zoe Ann's head hung down and she shook it. Mother pushed the call button. "Gini seemed upset too. Did the bad boys get to her?"

"Uh. uh. She got under a seat and swatted them away with a ruler. She screams real good, too."

Beth smiled and opened their door. "Good for her. Look, why don't you take her a cookie when you go down for your four o'clock play time?"

Zoe Ann slipped off her back pack. "Can't go there."

"Why? Are they going out or…" Mother saw tears streaming down her daughter's cheeks and dropped to her knees to face her. "Oh gosh, Baby. What's going on here?"

"It's her (sob) mother—says I can't come over anymore. We didn't do anything bad either."

"Uh, oh." Beth wiped her tears with a tissue. "Maybe Susan was offended by that Oppressor game you guys came up with. I'll talk to her. I think it'll be all right."

Zoe Ann sighed and nodded her head. Beth added, "Cheer up, the weekend is here. We'll find something fun to do and we'll start with milk and cookies."

With her daughter settled in at the kitchen table, Beth unpacked her back pack. "Look, they gave you a book on numbers games. Did you start learning arithmetic?"

"Uh, uh. They said there wasn't time. We had to see a movie."

"Really? Well, maybe because it was Friday. Was it for just for fun or did it teach something?"

Zoe Ann munched on a cookie and looked out the window. After a moment she said. "Not supposed to tell mom and dad they said."

Beth froze. Her old habit of teeth grinding returned. She composed herself and thought about a reply. With a big smile she said, "Oh that's just a game they play. They *know* you'll tell us all about it, but you're supposed to pretend you didn't."

Wide, innocent eyes looked up at her mother. "Really?"

"Yup, and I'm just dying to hear all about it."

"Well, it was a cartoon movie about boys and girls— kinda like the oppressor one but different."

"Sounds fascinating. What did the boys and girls do?"

"First, you can't call anyone boy or girl unless they say it's okay."

"Really? All right, but what went on in the movie?"

Zoe Ann squinched her face in thought. "It showed the different parts boys and girls have."

Teeth grinding resumed, but Beth forced a smile. "And, what did they do, dear?"

"The movie showed where boys and girls can touch and feel good. What do you think about that, Mommy?"

55

"What do I think?" Beth sighed. "I think we should consider home schooling."

TERRORISTS

Owen arrived early at the District Meeting determined, but without the megaphone. The board members were just getting seated behind a long table in front and he was able to slip into a seat in the front row. A woman in the next seat turned toward him. "Hello, I'm Martha Green. I have a fourth grader." She extended a hand and he shook it. "Are you going to ask a question?"

"Owen Wilson. I'd sure like to. I have a girl in kindergarten, but we may have to homeschool if they don't clear up the mess they've created."

"You mean they start their horrid propaganda *that* early?'

"I'm afraid so."

A man on her other side leaned forward. Martha pointed a thumb at him. "My husband, Mel."

With a squinched face. he said in a loud whisper, "They're trying to raise a generation of little Commies."

A woman on the raised table rapped a gavel. Owen smiled and whispered back. "I hear you."

The gavel rapper was a black woman wearing a dark gray suit and a blue tie. Her face was partly concealed by large round glasses that had a yellow tint. "Welcome everyone to the Brown County School Board public meeting. I am Chairperson Jackson. We will take questions from those who registered for them at the end of the meeting, time permitting."

A long and boring meeting followed with dissertations from various speakers on financing, total enrollment, the high quality of their new teachers, new adaptations to counter climate change and the glory filled life story of an assistant principal who retired last year. The only moment of interest came when they announced changing the name of Lincoln High School to Harriet Tubman High. That got a few boos.

Jackson looked at her watch. "We don't have much time left, but our first question comes from Martha Green."

A boy ran to her raised hand and handed her a microphone. Martha said, "I'll keep it short. I'd just like to know why my fourth grader knows new gender pronouns and wonders if he might be a girl but hasn't been taught multiplication?"

Jackson handed her microphone to a large bearded man next to her. His expression was one of disdain. "Well, of *course* that will be taught in due time. This is a changing world and we are dedicated to preparing our children for it."

"Won't basic math prepare them too?"

"Humph. Multiplication is in the schedule."

"Never mind, Mister. Mel and I taught him ourselves." Mixed laughter and applause scattered through the audience as Martha handed back the microphone and sat down.

"Next we have a Stella Marshall."

Stella was a tall mother in a yellow print dress. "Ahem, yes, that's me. My daughter Jenny is in third grade. She went from a happy girl to a depressed one who barely talks. We paid for a child psychologist, but what Jenny wouldn't tell us— mainly because *you* told her not to—was that she now believes she is an evil person. Your programs convinced her she is an oppressor of the poor and other races and they have no way to better themselves all because of her."

Another man on the dais leaned forward toward his microphone. "Is there a question in there, Marshall?"

Stella stood for a moment, her jaw trembling. "I—yes— why—why are you filling our children's minds with evil lies?"

His look became condescending and he gave a wry smile with a tilt of the head. "Ms. Marshall, our program must *expose* the *real* lies of the founders and bring enlightenment. Some children have difficulty because parents have programmed them beforehand. Problems with our children are always our concern, and I will refer our student to one of our qualified re-education specialists."

Stella was crying. Her husband rose to comfort her and took the microphone. Before he passed it down the row he said, "Not *your* child, Mister."

It was Owen's turn. "Owen Wilson. I have a girl in kindergarten. I have two questions. First, I have become aware that school boards all across America have suddenly introduced radical, new ideas about gender identity, racism, and hatred concerning everything our country has valued for centuries. What is the source of this material and who is spreading it around?"

Chairperson Jackson reached for her microphone. She looked down on him and shook her head. "Look, Mister Wilson, every year school boards evaluate academic information and we seek the *best* avenue forward to teach our children and prepare them for transitioning to global reality. Nonprofit humanitarian organizations like Resource Generation and the Ford Foundation have stepped into the breech to help this country. We are out of time but I'll allow your second question. Make it brief."

"So, elite billionaires took over education. Okay, you should know that our kindergarten girls were attacked by boys on the school bus last week. The boys were trying to touch the girls in the 'pleasure spots' your pornographic video showed them."

"Nonsense! How dare you?" She shook her head violently and pointed to two officers who moved toward Owen. "Take up your complaint with the principal. This meeting is over."

Owen shook a fist in the air and shouted, "I demand you stop showing our children pornography." Turning to the audience: "This is *child abuse*, folks."

The officers grabbed him, took away the microphone and began dragging him away. Jackson shouted back, "Consider yourself under arrest, homophobe!"

"Yeah? Consider yourself out of a job next election." There was scattered applause.

Outside, beside their squad car, the officers let go of Owen's arms. "So, am I really under arrest?"

One of the policemen spoke to his partner. "Mike, did you hear any charges?"

"They'll probably say disorderly conduct."

"But, he only raised his voice and told the truth about what happened."

"They really hate truth. They'll pass a law against it one day, but until they do, I guess we have to let him go."

The officers laughed, Mike added, "I have a third grader. Thanks for speaking up."

THE SERMON

Beth and Owen slipped into pews at Waters Alive Church and remained standing while the worship team belted out the tune called "Reckless Love." In a quiet moment between numbers, a woman shouted out in tongues and a man across the aisle stood up and spoke an interpretation: "The Lord says false prophets and deceiving spirits are upon us. Hold fast to my Word and you will stay in My truth."

After another worship song, Pastor Gary walked to the podium shaking his head. Owen whispered to his wife, "An elder in our Bible study told us that this sermon could get him fired."

The sermon title appeared on side mounted TV screens: "Delusional Living." Pastor Gary began, "I have to admit, I was kinda nervous about my message today, but that interpretation of God's word assures me I'm right on point. Look, if you want a pastor who coddles you, there's plenty of them out there."

"We tend to deceive ourselves all the time. Last week I had to get up at seven for an eight thirty meeting, and I set my alarm for a few minutes early just to be really sure. When it sounded, I turned it off, yawned, and told myself: 'It's not even seven. I'll just close my eyes for another ten minutes.' Right." Scattered snickers went around the congregation.

"You guessed it. I woke up an hour later. Deceptions are often based on what we would *like* the truth to be while ignoring the clear evidence of reality. They can be just dumb, like mine, or truly evil. Jeremiah seventeen, verse nine tells us: 'The heart is deceitful above all things and desperately wicked.' That's not a reassuring commentary on us humans, is it?"

"If we can't even be honest with ourselves, it should come as no surprise that others may not be truthful toward *us*, especially if they will gain from their deception." Gary looked over at his family sitting in the first row. "When my wife saw my sermon title, she asked me if I still had my Teaching Certificate—just in case."

He chuckled. "I think she thought I was going to talk politics, but that would have to be a ten-part series instead of one sermon." Audience laughter. "Unfortunately, I'm going to talk about something even riskier—religious delusions."

Gary began to walk back and forth along the front edge of the stage. "I'll give you the bottom line first. The one and only almighty God has given us a path of truth and life. He even wrote it down for us, but if we make up our *own* contradictory truth instead, we create a path of destruction for ourselves. What they call relativism is no truth at all, and even secular philosophy defines truth as existing independent of human thoughts."

"As children, our parents directed our lives and assigned us things we didn't want to do. Knowing what's best, good parents teach responsibility, kindness toward others and obedience. As normal kids, however, we kept trying to find ways to do what *we* want instead." He opened his hands. "Remember?"

"The truth is, our selfish little hearts haven't changed. God, in His infinite wisdom and love, left us His Word to guide us and awaken our spirits to control our deceitful hearts with His one and only truth. When that happens, we accept His Son as our Lord and Savior and He rewards us with salvation and everlasting life. No amount of money can buy a gift that precious."

"However, many men resist His truth and prefer to invent new religions they themselves control. Romans 1:24 warns us not to worship the *created* rather than the Creator. Baal was one of the first of those created gods, which actually serve as shells for deceiving demon spirits. Outside of the Judeo-Christian faith, we have religions based on things like self-awareness, or the Hindu belief that we are in a dream of God, or religions simply based on man's own knowledge."

"More disturbing to me, however, are the deceptive, Bible-twisting religions that have sprung up since Jesus. They have two things in common. First, they reject the inerrant truth of the Bible and Jesus as God. Second, they claim to have discovered new, secret truths and revere an all-wise founder who wrote a new book of faith for them. The largest is Islam which worships the Moon God, Ilah, now called Al-Ilah or Allah. They seek to convert the world by killing or enslaving us non-believers and think they are doing the will of their god."

"Far more subtle and complex is Mormonism. They believe that man is inherently good and can be promoted to godship by good works and given a planet to rule. Each planet, including ours, has a god appointed by the ruling gods. They revere a person's feelings of right and wrong as testimony of spiritual revelation without checking them against the Bible. They also think Father God began as a human being and that Jesus attained godhood through obedience and devotion. Oops!"

"Psalm four, two says 'How long will you have delusions and follow false gods?' I could name many other religions and cults, but let us not drink the Kool Aid. What do they all have in common? They are man-made religions, designed to suit themselves. It should be easy to spot them for what they are, yet many are deceived."

Gary looked down and shook his head. "Now I'm coming to the gut-wrenching part that will offend a lot of people. The *most* disturbing thing to me is what has happened to some good Christian denominations over time."

Beth took Owen's hand, leaned toward him and whispered. "Susie told me Gary once said some bad things about Catholics."

Pastor gripped the podium with both hands and leaned forward. "I know we are in delicate territory now since we all have friends in other denominations, but there are two things I'm *not* going to do today. I'm not going to criticize things they do like fancy liturgy, and I'm not going to name individuals— well, maybe just one." Murmurs went through the congregation.

"Matthew five, twenty-two makes it quite clear that accusing or ridiculing our Christian brothers and sisters *without cause* shall put us in danger of hell fire. God knows how to keep our family discussions calm, doesn't He?" Soft laughter.

"On the other hand, when our Christian family is deceived and wanders from God's truth, it is our *duty* to help turn them back to God's ordained path. He has not changed since He created this universe, and He gave us the knowledge we need in this book." Gary picked up the Bible. "Its name stands for Basic Information Before Leaving Earth. The Lord did not say that we can pick and choose parts to follow and parts to reject."

Pastor took a deep breath and resumed strolling around the stage. "When I was a kid, a Catholic friend told me that only the Catholics go to Heaven. Even then I thought that was funny, but apparently, things have not changed. Pope Francis recently declared that 'It is not possible to find Jesus outside the Catholic church.' Note that Popes are regarded as infallible."

"Seeming to contradict that, I read a report quoting the Pope that left me speechless—I think the word is 'gob-smacked.' I still hope the report was wrong. On September eleventh, 2013, he was quoted as saying: 'non-believers will be forgiven by God and go to Heaven if they follow their conscience.' Talk about denying the word of God, huh? Perhaps responding to protests from that remark, in 2019 he affirmed a statement claiming that 'Evangelical Protestants cannot really be defined as Christians.' Got it?"

"Many Christians are falling away from God's truth en masse, becoming casualties of a culture that celebrates pluralism, relativism, and sex without boundaries. To hide their sins, they claim that there are no moral absolutes. Notice the admonition in Romans one, eighteen: 'For the wrath of God is revealed from heaven against all ungodliness and the wickedness of men, who suppress the truth by their wickedness.' God's meaning is clear: do not pretend your lies are the truth."

Gary paused for a moment, looked skyward and mumbled something inaudible. "So much for God's plan, huh? Folks, God does not offer us His opinion of the month. He and His Word are *forever* truth. In Acts four, twelve, God refers to Jesus and states 'there is no other name under heaven given among men by which we must be saved.' Since God is the *only* one doing the saving, maybe we better stick to *His* plan, huh?" Scattered Amens.

"We well-intentioned human beings like to go along to get along, as they say, but being a nice guy doesn't get us to Heaven, and one is not moral because he *claims* to be. Without getting political, I think it's safe to say our society has been in a moral decline. Sadder yet is the fact that some Christian denominations have, in effect, redacted portions of the Bible to accommodate our immoral society. For instance, many now perform same sex marriages.

"I believe the signs clearly point to our being in the end times, and First Timothy, four begins with the revelation that in the last days, some of us will abandon the faith, follow deceiving spirits and things taught by demons. Near the spot in New York where our nation was dedicated by George Washington, we have a golden bull, and nearby they recently erected a copy of the Syrian arch that led to the kingdom of Baal.

"Besides that, China is preparing for war and their leader could be the Antichrist. The seven-year tribulation would end in 2028, forty jubilee periods and 2000 years after Jesus crucifixion.

"Friends, the desire for sin comes with self-delusion. We are not free to make up new religions to include those sins like the worship of sex, money, climate, 'wokeism' or technology. We either believe in God's unblurred truth or not. In Genesis, God tells us he made man male and female to be joined together as one flesh and to be fruitful and multiply. There is no plan B."

The pastor returned to the podium and exhaled a big breath. Background organ music begins. "I could go on with many more examples, but I'm sure you get the point. I don't intend to conclude on a shaky-head note of despair. Instead, I am giving you a call to arms—spiritual arms to speak God's truth to this world of the flesh. When you do, you will be persecuted. Good. Accept that with joy, but talk gently to your friends and family members with love and understanding. Do not condemn anything but the deception they have fallen for. Teach."

"Today, I hereby appoint each one of you, my faithful brothers and sisters, to be saviors of the Bride of Christ and our world, one person at a time. I call upon you to boldly speak God's Word to the people of our troubled planet. You are anointed to be ministers of His truth. As Paul said in Second Timothy three twelve, you should expect persecution. Take delight in that, for they persecuted Jesus and your reward in Heaven will be great and Jesus will be returning soon. Put on the full armor of God and go forth boldly and without fear, for He will always be with you. God bless you all."

A standing ovation followed with shouts of "Praise God," Halleluiahs and Amens.

DÉTENTE

Enjoying an afternoon in the park, Beth spun her daughter around on the merry go-round. Another rider slipped a bit and screamed so Beth slowed it down. "Are you getting dizzy?"

"Uh, uh." Zoe Ann hopped off and staggered a few steps and laughed. "I want to go on the teeter-totters but you're too big to be on the other side."

Beth took her hand as they headed toward them. "Maybe we'll find someone the right size for you."

"Okay. I like to bounce at the top and…" A white curly-haired dog with random black patches ran up to Zoe Ann. She dropped to her knees and began exchanging face kisses. "Its Muddy! Gini must be here somewhere."

Beth noticed the dog was trailing a leash so she picked up the end and searched down the path he came from. "Ah, there's Missus Adams on a bench."

"Mommy, go talk to her. Maybe I can play with Gini again."

Beth sat down on a nearby park bench to make eye contact with her daughter. "I don't think that's a good idea, Darlin.' Susan won't answer my calls or texts." Zoe Ann returned a big frown. "But here's a plan that might work. You go and return her dog and apologize for the oppressor game that upset her so much. I'll stay here and pretend I'm not watching."

"Okay, but Muddy sometimes pulls on the leash."

Beth put Zoe Ann's hand on the leash a short way from the collar. "Here's what you do. Let him know you are in charge. Walk straight down the path. Keep the leash relaxed but if he pulls to the side, give him a little upward tug and say 'nope, nope.' He'll learn to obey you."

Zoe Ann made her way confidently down the path, fist making two successful corrections and stood before Gini's mother. She was reading a magazine and didn't notice her. Gini was on a swing not far away. "Uh, Missus Adams…"

"Uh, huh," came from behind the magazine.

"Muddy got away, but I brought him back."

Susan slammed the magazine down, grabbed the leash and tied it to the arm of the bench. "Well, thank you. He's a bad dog."

Gini had stopped swinging but she looked on, her eyes wide. Zoe Ann knelt down, put one arm around Muddy to give her strength, and looked up with an imploring face. "Missus Adams. I am so, *so* sorry about that game that upset you. They taught us those words in school and I still don't even know what they mean—honest."

Susan looked down at the two of them, fighting back a smile. "You look like Muddy begging for a treat."

Zoe Ann pulled two fists up below her chin. "Gini is my best friend ever--*ever*! Can't I play with her again? Please?"

Susan's smile broke through. "Well, I'll allow that you didn't really know what you were doing, but if I grant that wish, you'll have to pay me reparations."

"Repair—uh, what?"

"Reparations is payment for your wrongs. Agree to them, and I'll let you see Gini again."

Zoe Ann's face lit up with hope. "Oh, yes, but I only have about fifteen dollars saved. Is that enough?"

"I don't want your money, dear, but I see you are an artist with great talent. Promise to paint me a picture of Muddy and all is forgiven."

She leaped to her feet. "Oh, yes, *yes*! I'll paint the best picture *ever*. You'll see."

Susan waved her daughter over. The girls held each other and jumped up and down. Beth grinned. Muddy barked.

THE NARRATIVE

"Hi Honey. I'm home." Owen put his jacket on a hook by the door.

Beth bounded in to embrace him and land a kiss. "Well, look at you. I thought I was going to have to visit you in jail."

"Nope, not yet." He chuckled. "But I think that was more freedom-of-speech than they could handle. I just hope I did some good." He headed for the living room. "Now I think I'll rest a bit with some cold water. I have a text coming in."

Beth said, "Just sit. I'll get us both some." In a moment she returned and sat on the couch beside him. "Cold water with clunky cubes and a lemon slice for my hero. Is the text important?"

"It's from Isaiah. He wrote, 'Way to go, Dad.' I guess he saw the TV coverage."

"Right, but each channel gave a different slant. I DVR'd a couple. Wanna see?" Owen took a sip of water and nodded.

Beth picked up the remote. "Okay, News Box showed all the questions and responses without editing." She showed the clip that ended with a reporter commenting on the bravery of parents. "See," giggle. "You didn't need my megaphone, did you? Now watch what the mainstream media showed at six o'clock."

The edited clips were preceded by an announcer saying, "If you needed more evidence of why the DOJ is concerned about domestic terrorism, watch this."

The first woman spoke, her voice distressed: "I'd just like to know why my fourth grader knows new gender pronouns and wonders if he might be a girl?" (cut) A close up of her shaking fist. The response: "This is a changing world and we are dedicated to preparing our children for it."

Owen said, "They cut the part where she points out the deficiency in teaching math."

The video flashed to a woman raising her arms and imploring, "Your program has convinced my daughter she is an oppressor of the poor." (cut) The response: "Ms. Marshal, our program believes in exposing the founder's lies and bringing enlightenment. Some children have difficulty because *parents* have programmed them with slaveholder propaganda beforehand."

Now Owen was shown starting from his second remark about boys molesting girls on the school bus after seeing a school video. The response: "Nonsense! How dare you."

The vid moved in to show his upraised arm and amplified his voice. "This is child abuse, folks."

"Consider yourself under arrest, homophobe."

A shot of the police grabbing him and him trying to twist away, then the edited clip, "Consider yourself out of a job."

The moderator commented. "Sounds like a personal threat, doesn't it?"

Finally, an outside shot behind the police car showing upraised and flailing arms. Beth asked, "What was that about?"

Owen chuckled. "Sure looks like I'm resisting arrest, doesn't it?"

"Were you?"

"No, the police were wishing me well and helping me get my jacket back on."

SCIENCE

A lie told often enough becomes the truth.

Vladimir Lenin

Isaiah was almost late arriving at the lecture hall. He slipped into the end seat of the second row just as the bell rang. Earth Science was a popular course and he had survived the first two weeks without asking any questions. Today would be different.

Professor Arnoult was not wearing his usual plaid jacket but a camouflage shirt and army boots as he moved to the lectern. "Good morning, class. We are moving on from plate tectonics and earthquakes to the atmosphere—from things we cannot control to things we *must* control. This is one area of Earth Science I'm sure you have all heard about—climate change, global warming and our role in managing it."

He wiggled his podium around and flipped open his notes. "With so many press reports on this subject, I'll first try to clear up the misinformation out there."

A woman behind Isaiah spoke up. "Oh, yes. *Please!*"

"I'll start by asking if anyone has questions." Isaiah's hand shot up. He pointed to him. "Yes?"

"Professor, what is it that causes earth's climate to cycle from ice ages to poles free of ice?" The woman giggled.

"Well, I didn't expect that question, but those are slow natural changes over many thousands of years brought on by the tilt in our axis and solar activity. Read up on chapter four." He looked out at the audience. "Questions on the more recent and *pertinent* changes?"

"Sir, a follow up?" Isaiah called out. "What direction are we heading into right now: Ice Age or Polar Melting?"

Arnoult gave Isaiah a self-assured nod and pointed a finger at him. "There's a fair question, and the answer is it is up to us, isn't it? Mans' recent activity has taken over the forces of nature and our reckless burning of fossil fuel has caused dramatic increases in CO_2 and global temperatures."

Feigning shock Isaiah responded. "Wow, what can we do to save us all?" Another giggle from behind.

Arnoult looked over his audience. "Energy must be taken away from irresponsible private interests. Only nationalization and conversion to solar and wind will save humanity."

Isaiah remained standing. "Ah, thank goodness. With the climate controlled, breezy, and cloudless, those Chinese devices will save us from our carbon footprint and lower our CO_2 from the 0.04% where we are now. Gosh, without them, we might even boil away like Mars with its 95% CO_2 atmosphere."

The professor gave him an angry squint and emitted a hiss. He strode to the other side of the room and pointed to another raised hand. Isaiah felt a gentle touch on his shoulder. A female voice whispered in his ear. "He won't call on you again. Do you have another question?"

He turned around to the pretty face of a woman with curly blonde hair and bright green eyes sparkling with enthusiasm. "Sure do. I wrote my biggest zinger down."

She took his note, gave his shoulder a quick double squeeze and scooted five seats away to an empty chair. Arnoult went on at length with a lecture demonizing fossil fuel and praising solar farms and electric-only transportation.

When he swaggered back to the lectern, he saw the enthusiastic waving hand. "All right. Just one more question. What is it, little lady?"

"I read that our NASA satellites have been recording extremely accurate average global temperatures for half a century. Tell us how much global warming they show."

Arnoult looked like he had just been slapped. "I, uh—there are *many* gauges and computer projections of global temperature—not sure what you're referring to."

"Well, Sir," she stood up grinning and declared in a loud voice. "The truth is, that measured to one one-hundredth of a degree and even with our proliferation of fossil fuel burning, there has been *absolutely no* change in average global temperature since 1982."

"Misinformation!" Enraged, he pointed a finger and shouted, "You right wing twits choose to ignore glacier melting, sea level rising and our endangered polar bears. Read the booklets in your course plan."

He took a deep breath, composed himself and closed his folder. "No more questions. We're done for today."

The students began to leave, but a female voice from the crowd called out, "Lots more happy polar bears these days."

The woman came back to Isaiah. They exchanged a fist bump and she handed back his question. "Hi, I'm Patti. That turned out to be a fun lecture, huh?"

Picking up his backpack, he replied, "Sure was. I'm Isaiah. Can I buy you a cup of coffee?"

"You may." Her grand smile gave him a tingly feeling in his chest." She added, "But, we better not go to the Student Lounge right now. They might stone us."

He laughed. "Okay, so it's the Daily Grind off campus—and more expensive coffee."

On their way off campus, they waited for a traffic light to change. She looked deeply into his eyes. "You'll discover my passions are simple: Sumatra dark coffee, truth and those who speak it—and, most of all, Jesus."

COFFEE

As they walked up to the Daily Grind, Patti scooted in a gate surrounding the outdoor tables and pointed. "Ooh, that's the one." She motioned to Isaiah. "Go around to the hostess and ask for an outside table."

He did as he was told and returned with the hostess who said, "There are two left. Your choice."

Isaiah saw his friend sitting at a corner table for two, nicely shaded. "I think I'll take the one with the cute blonde."

She laughed. "You're on your own with that one."

He went over to her shaking his head with a grin. She looked up. "Well, see, this other couple was about to grab the best table."

"But now it's *ours*."

Patti gave him a wide smile. "Right—ours." She pointed her finger at him. I'll bet you have a nickname."

"Sure, call me Izzy."

The waitress came out, apparently briefed by the hostess. "I hope he isn't bothering you."

Patti produced a fake look of anger. "Oh, he *is*, Jessica—something *awful*—but I just can't help asking for more."

The waitress snickered. "Patti, right? You're usually here with several women. What can I get you two?"

Patti gave her a hopeful look. "Sumatra dark. Did you make your Irish scones today?"

"A fresh batch just came out of the oven."

"Perfect. We'll take an order."

Isaiah said, "A small latte for me." When the waitress left, he asked, "Sounds like you're familiar with this place."

"Uh huh. We girls from Youths for Freedom meet here all the time. You might want to join. Say, that was brilliant what you did in class. I wouldn't have had the courage to speak up like I did without your going first."

"Thanks, but I'll bet we just got a D-minus for the year."

"Probably, but I think I'll have my grade made into a lapel pin." She gave him another smile and a softness came into her tone. "Ignoring accusations and simply asking questions makes the other person evaluate their own position. Jesus did that a lot."

Scones and coffee arrived. After a bite, Isaiah held one up. "Say, these are delicious. You know, I'll bet the Pharisees knew it was just fine to heal on the Sabbath, right? Arnoult reminds me of them—ignoring truth and protecting their man-made control narrative."

"Absolutely," Patti squinted at him. "But, do you think Arnoult really knows global warming is a hoax designed to justify nationalizing the energy industry?"

"He's too smart not to. There are only two types who like to fear-monger a hoax like that—the liars who stand to gain personally, and those whom they have frightened and deceived."

"So true, and we didn't even get to ask about the four government sponsored papers in 2015 showing computer projections of runaway CO_2 in five years."

"Yeah, Mother Nature sure laughed at their projections. There was no significant increase by 2020, but they still quote the studies claiming that 95% of climate scientists predict skyrocketing CO_2. Hey, that's a good question for next class."

Patti pointed a finger at him. "And, amazingly, no media ever reported the *thirty thousand* scientists who signed a paper disclaiming man's influence in climate change."

"It's all about political control. They're fear mongers wanting to control industry and they use carbon emissions as an excuse. Whoever controls a nation's energy controls the nation. Solar, wind and EVs are mainly a payoff to China."

She pointed at the lone biscuit on the plate. "Say, do you think Jessica gave us *three* scones as a test?"

Isaiah snatched the last one and she returned an indignant pout. He broke off a small piece, popped it into his mouth, but extended the scone to her mouth. She took a bite, doe eyes aimed at his heart. "Ours," he said.

STORIES IN ART

The next two years flew by at the Wilsons. Owen's experience and leadership led him to be Crew Chief coordinator and he now has a good salary at their new location. Beth is working full time at a pre-school, the perfect hours for her to be home for Zoe Ann's school bus arrival. Isaiah remained at the state college, making the voice of truth heard with, of course, Patti.

One afternoon, Beth went to her daughter's room. "Hi, darling. You're not playing with Gini today?"

She looked over her easel. "No, Ma, I'm working on learning watercolors.

Beth came around to look. "Gosh, you're not painting over your mother's drawing, are you?"

"'Course not, Ma, I made a photocopy on your printer to color in." She pointed to one of Ann's drawings which covered a whole wall in her room. "It's that one. Her mother's drawing showed an old woman handing an American flag to a girl as they climbed up a hill together."

"Your mother was very talented. I'm glad to see she passed that on to you."

"When I was a child, I didn't understand that her drawings told a story."

Beth snickered at "when I was a child," but asked "So, what story does *this* one tell?"

"Don't you see? Grandma wants to carry America to the top, but she's asking her granddaughter to take our country the rest of the way."

Beth put a hand on her shoulder and bent down to look. "I see that. Are you changing something?"

"Not much, but the flag was begging me to make the colors come out, and see, now the girl is turning to run up ahead. I put up the final one on the wall already."

Beth stood back up and surveyed the wall covered with Ann's pictures. "Ah, you're making them all prettier—sort of like a coloring book."

Zoe Ann giggled and got up, her tone condescending. "No, Ma." She went to the wall and pointed. "Mother Ann told me to draw the *next* picture."

"Mother Ann…" Beth looked at another drawing beside the original. "Did *you* draw this?"

"Of course. It's what happens in the end."

Beth took the sketch off the wall to study it. The drawing was almost as good as the original and showed the girl standing on top of the mountain, proudly holding the American flag she had planted. "Zoe *Ann,* I'm so amazed, Honey. You could fill an entire gallery when you're finished."

"I dunno. Watercolor wrinkles the paper."

"Honey, I'm sure they make a special paper for this. I'll stop off at the art store tomorrow and get some for you. I wouldn't want to see your talent wasted on warped paper."

Zoe Ann grinned. "So, you like my stuff?"

"I love them, Darlin. Did you do any more 'next step' pictures?"

"Uh, I'm working on another one, but I'm not sure about it. Mother Ann wants me to think about things, you know."

Beth put her hand on her chest. "Oh, that's just precious. What drawing did you start?"

Her daughter pointed to a picture of a man and woman kissing. Beth said, "Uh, oh. What did you come up with?"

"I don't know if my mother would like this or not." She rummaged through some papers and handed a drawing to Beth. It pictured the couple standing next to a pastor. Clearly. they were getting married.

Beth gave her daughter a hug. "Oh, Darling, I think Mother Ann would say it's absolutely perfect."

FILTHY LUCRE

Patti chuckled and looked up at Isaiah as they walked toward a class. "I can't believe I'm doing this, even on a dare."

"Somebody has to ask the right questions, don't you think?"

"You have to protect me if I do, Izzy."

"No problem. I have two steel rulers and I took a class in martial arts. I even have a black belt."

"You earned a Black Belt?"

"Nah, I'm just wearing a black belt."

That got him a shoulder swat. "Look, this class we signed up for is called Society, Justice and Equity. I think they'll be teaching us how to make protest signs and bang drums."

"And for extra credit, students can burn down a Federal courthouse." Isaiah held the door open for her with a grin. "There you go. We're early. It's a small classroom so there shouldn't be too many enemy combatants."

"All right. I'm not going to worry. Maybe the biggest casualty will be my grade point average, but let's sit by the door just in case we have to make a run for it."

The first four to arrive were black—friends laughing at a joke. Patti whispered. "Uh, oh. Do you wanna borrow some dark makeup?"

He finger-pointed back. "You *are* gonna get us in trouble, aren't you?"

The rest of the class that arrived included a racial mixture so they calmed down. Patti said, "Sorry. I'm just nervous."

Finally, an overweight man walked in, hairy arms protruding from a khaki shirt. He put a briefcase down and sat on a wide stool. He studied his class through extremely narrow gold glasses. "Welcome to Social Justice, everyone. I am instructor Dominik Yurchenko."

He took out a small clipboard from his bag and gestured for one in the first row to take it. "Everyone's name should be on the sheet. Sign beside yours for attendance. I'll start with a simple question. It won't count for your grade. If you would join a protest march for a cause you believed in, raise your hand."

Isaiah raised his and looked at Patti with an enthusiastic nod. She raised hers and whispered, "Since you put it that way."

Their instructor raised his plump arm with a finger pointing upward. "As the saying goes, we live in the best of times and the worst of times. Worst because greed, inequity and racism reign, best because we can change the system of oppression that brought it about." His hand became a fist.

Dominick stood up nodding his head. "Our first lesson today will be to gain an understanding of how our oppressive system began and exposing the lies we find in our history books. Only then will we be able to see the glowing path leading to a new and just government—a new order."

He began to stroll back and forth in front of the students. "In sixteen nineteen, the white supremacists here went from aggressive conquers to slave masters. They founded a country on capitalism, greed and the racial oppression that still exists today."

His eyes fixed on Isaiah for a moment who promptly raised his hand. "Uh, Professor Yurchenko…"

"Thank you for the promotion," he smiled. "But just call me Dominick in this class."

"All right. Dominick, after we have risen up and destroyed America's capitalistic system, what form of new order government should we replace it with?"

Their instructor opened his hands and lifted his head as though he were getting divine inspiration. He spoke to the ceiling with a beatific smile. "Our new order will be one in which we contribute according to our ability and receive according to our needs. It will be one in which everyone will be at peace in equitable submission."

"Sir, that is a quote from Karl Marx. Is the New Order you envision the same as his?"

Dominick took a step backward and glowered at Isaiah. "No one has yet achieved the complete utopia that is possible in the world to come. In future lessons I will explain how this beautiful vision will be brought into reality."

Isaiah opened up his hands to mimic the instructor. "Do we have a name for this new form of government yet?"

"Ah, names can be misunderstood and attacked. The New Order will name itself, for it will reign as a higher power-- higher than anything the world has ever seen."

It was Patti's turn to bravely stand up. "Oh, that's so beautiful, Dominick."

"I know," he said, the beatific smile returning.

She clasped her hands together and boldly declared, "I see it too. We will all work to form this new government--one founded on worshiping that higher power, the Word, and the Spirit of our loving God."

The students responded with boos and moans. One threw a ball of crumpled paper at her but Isaiah swatted it back at the thrower with his ruler. "Now, now," Dominick pointed at him. "We're not here to attack the ignorant, but to educate them."

As Patti sat back down, she glanced at the scowling faces turned toward her, but noted there was one woman in the back corner giving her a smiling thumbs up.

The instructor returned to his podium. "Actually, I'm glad that came up. In this course we will show that the root problem of all humankind has been false beliefs in gods and others whom they hope would solve the world's problems. History shows this has led to false hopes in a nonexistent deity, and to kings, fascist rulers and even racist slave owners."

He leaned forward to make squinting eye contact, darting from one student to the next. "In the New World Order, we will achieve equity, fairness, submission and thus, happiness for all. This new state will understand each need and respond with justice. Eventually there will be no dissenters."

Patti whispered to Isaiah, "Cause they'll either be dead or in work camps."

He whispered back. "He wants to replace the worship of God with his idea of a patriotism—a fascist state."

The Asian woman waved her hand and got the nod. "Dominick, would there be democracy?"

"Of course, and with only one party, the brutal fighting you see today will disappear and the people will elect one enlightened person to lead them."

"I've lived in that world, Dominick."

"No, the true New Order has yet to be created."

"Oh, but the government you describe *does* exist. It is one founded on complete deception and I am its refugee. I escaped from North Korea."

THE BLUES

Gini and Zoe Ann walked and skipped down the street with Beth keeping a watchful eye not far behind. Zoe Ann said, "*This time I'm going higher than you, you'll see.*"

Gini did a spin around and grinned. "Na uh! You get scared when the swing bounces."

"Am not. I'll bounce higher than you."

"Nah, you're a scaredy cat. Just wa…" Gini froze at the entrance to the park and turned to her friend. "I can't go in there."

Zoe Ann searched the park but just saw children playing. She grinned. "Uh, oh. Is that tyrannosaurus back again?"

"No, I'm serious. There's a white policeman."

Beth caught up with them. "What's the problem, Gini?"

"There!" She pointed to an officer. "There's usually none of them around."

"Oh, Gini, last week they caught someone dealing drugs near here. I guess they added more protection. You're not afraid of policemen, are you?"

"Carla and Jim said they'll shoot you if you're black and it looks like you're running away."

Beth squatted down and searched her worried face. "Let's talk about this. You can come in with me and we'll sit on that bench right here near the fence."

Gini let Beth take her hand and they went in. Zoe Ann just looked on with a puzzled expression. Beth gestured toward the officer. "Look, he's playing a game of horse with the older kids and some are black. Do you think he looks dangerous?"

"I can see his gun."

"They're all supposed to have guns, Gini."

Zoe Ann piped up. "That's to scare bad guys away."

Gini looked down and shook her head, unconvinced. Beth had an idea. "Do you know either of the black boys?"

She flick-pointed. "Yeah, in the red shirt--that's JJ, Rona's brother. He's in sixth grade."

"Great. Looks like the game is over." Beth stood up and waved at him. "Hi, JJ, can I ask you something?"

He came over with a puzzled look. "Sorry, do I know you?" Then a quick glance to her companion. "Oh, hi, Gini."

Beth shook his hand. "I'm Beth, Zoe Ann's mom. Gini is worried about something. Maybe you could help?"

He shrugged. "Sure, what?"

"Gini said she's afraid of white policemen—thinks they shoot you when you turn away."

JJ released a huge belly laugh. "Oh God, that is such BS." He bent over to look Gini in the eye. "Look, kid, that's

97

just not true. It's a lie made up for politics—maybe to get votes or something. Who told you that?"

"Carla."

"Yeah, she's an activist, but she shouldn't be scaring kids your age." He looked over his shoulder and waved. "Say, Benni! Officer Benjamin. Can you come over a sec?"

Benni strode toward them with long, bold steps. Gini scrunched against Beth. JJ said, "Someone told Gini here that white policemen shoot black people. The only thing I've seen you shoot are hoops and you can't even shoot those."

Benni laughed at JJ and pointed a finger at him. "Yeah? Just wait 'till next time." He went down on his haunches to talk to Gini, her face now contorted with fear. Beth began a gentle shoulder massage.

Policeman Benni studied the child's expression for a few moments then sat on the pavement cross-legged so he looked up at her. "Gosh, Gini, it hurts me really bad that you would think that."

Zoe Ann thought she'd help. "Carla showed us a video on her TV."

Benni nodded. "First, I want to say that I love this neighborhood and everyone in it—and that includes you, Gini. I would never, *ever* hurt anyone on purpose. My job is to protect you from the bad guys, not help them."

He gave Gini a broad smile full of compassion. She relaxed. "Next, I'll admit that some cops have made mistakes, but even then, I don't believe they intended to do harm in the first place. The last news clip I saw was a man getting out of his car and running away when he was shot. Is that the one you saw?"

She nodded and Benni shook his head. "Yeah, thought so. Most news programs edited out the part where the guy started shooting at us *first* before he ran away."

Gini stiffened up. "Really?"

"Yup, really. In fact, if you and your friends want to see the whole video clip, you can be my guests at police headquarters and I'll personally show it to you."

"Gosh, Carla too?"

"Especially Carla. I'll set up a time with your parents. I'm giving you a special privilege pass. He handed Beth a card. "Look, Gini, I just want you to know I really care about you."

Gini hopped off the bench and gave him a hug. "Thank you, mister police-cop Benni."

He returned the hug, stood up and grinned at Beth. "Well, I gotta go. Hope to see you at the station soon."

Gini shot Zoe Ann a challenging look. "Race you to the swings, chicken-girl."

SUPREMACISTS

By this time, Isaiah and Patti were affectionate soulmates and their antics in class were well known. Today, they boldly sat in the student lounge chatting over inferior coffee.

Isaiah leaned toward her with a grin. "Yesterday I got called in to see my student advisor."

"Let me guess. The university wants you to take a class in anger management and submission."

"You're close. No, his advice was to stop acting self-important and being disruptive in my classes He reminded me that students could be expelled for hate speech."

"Hate speech? Well," she chuckled, "the good news is you made our elitist faculty take notice. Did you tell him what you really thought of his admonition?"

"No, but I did get a nasty twitch in my middle finger." Patti laughed. "Actually, I thanked him for his advice but said I would have to think about whether I should give up my first amendment rights—told him I'd get back to him on that."

Patti said, "Here's some news. I got kicked off the soccer team." Isaiah returned a sympathetic "oh" look. "Yeah, they said everyone had to kneel down in honor of BLM. I told them I only kneel before God."

"Darn right. You should have a legal case there."

"Nah, too much trouble." She leaned toward him and whispered. "But guess what, Izzy? I cracked their code."

"Code?"

"The secret to understanding what elite Marxists are up to. They always accuse others of what *they* are actually doing."

"Oh, yeah, like 'Russian collusion' while they were the ones taking in millions from them and other countries."

"Uh huh—and like racist while *they* were actually the slave owners and voted against giving blacks their rights in the sixties. They call us Nazis while *their* plan is a totalitarian government transforming citizens into their obedient subjects."

"I see your point. When they say *they're* saving democracy they really mean they're saving one party rule and destroying our free Republic."

Patti glowered at him. "I saw that. You thought I wouldn't notice you stealing the rest of my doughnut."

"What? You little sneak. You finished *mine*!"

She gave him a sparkly eyed grin. "Heh, heh. Perfect. See, that's *just* how it works." They laughed.

Three students came in talking loudly. The slurring of their speech suggested the influence of hops. Suddenly, one stopped and pointed at them. "Hey!" Patti and Isaiah looked up with calm curiosity. "*Those* two," he ranted. "They're the racist, white-supremacist dirt bags."

One man threw a crumpled sandwich wrapper at them, but Isaiah caught it before it collided with Patti. He tossed it back.

The lead guy came closer to press his case. "You two don't belong here. How about you quit college and join the Proud Boys, huh?"

Isaiah smiled. "If there is something you'd like to discuss, please have a seat. I'll buy you coffee."

He leaned in close to Isaiah's face. Yup, beer breath. "I ain't talkin' to no trash like you."

"Uh, how about if I throw in a doughnut?"

Beer breath drew back his hand to strike but his companion grabbed his arm and head-nodded toward a campus policeman by the door. "Okay, but if I see you two around here again, you'll pay—got it?"

The three turned to walk out. Isaiah called to their backs. "I'll have my two cents ready."

Patti grinned at her boyfriend. "Maybe next time--the Daily Grind, right?"

They were surprised to find a slender girl standing next to them. Her straight blonde hair hung below her shoulders. Light blue eyes pleaded for attention. "Can I have that offer to talk?" she said.

Patti pulled out an empty chair. "Of course. I'm Patti. This is Izzy. Have a seat."

"Oh, thanks." She sat and glanced from one to the other. "I'm Emma—a freshman—no, you're supposed to say First Year Student, aren't you? I came here to study graphic arts, but coming from a small town in Iowa, this place confuses me."

Isaiah nodded. "A bit of culture shock, huh?"

"I guess. It doesn't seem like I'm in America anymore."

Isaiah got up. "Our advice comes with coffee and a free doughnut. What kind do you like?"

"Cinnamon crumb."

Patti said, "Good choice. Don't think you're alone. Those guys are just loud and confused. They've swallowed the lie and enjoy the virtue signaling that goes with it."

Emma sighed. "What hurts the most is this racist thing. In my high school Blacks, Filipinos, Asian and Latinos were all mixed in—gays, too, and no one even thought about it. A Black student won a state award in a music competition, and our class president was Korean. We didn't even have any real cliques— well, except for the cheerleaders." Eye roll. "Anyway, I *resent* being called racist by people who don't even know me."

Sensing tears were coming, Patti put her hand on hers. "Of course, you're not. They're trying to scare you so you'll submit to their ideology. They claim the moral high ground, but it is a complete deception. Stay strong, girl. We're with you."

Isaiah returned with the doughnuts and coffee. "I think it helps to look at the big picture."

Emma held up her pastry. "Thanks, Izzy."

"To get an overview, imagine yourself in a plane," His hand swooped down, then "flew" over the table. "You are banking left and looking down at the whole landscape."

Patti gave Emma a little poke, "Izzy is going to take flying lessons this summer. So masculine, huh?"

Isaiah pointed back. "Be nice or you won't get a ride."

Emma chuckled. "My older sister just got her Commercial Pilot's License, so I *know* it's not just for men."

"Okay, okay." Isaiah held out his palms. "The big picture was a metaphor. Let's get serious and look at what is behind all this."

"You mean why they shout insults at strangers?"

"In this country, it all goes back a hundred years or so. The evil ones seeking power and wealth decided to follow the plan of a historic general who had a scheme to bring down a larger adversary by patient, *progressive* victories."

Emma shook half a cinnamon doughnut at him. "So, that's why they call themselves Progressives?"

"I think so, but they began as Fabian Socialists. Anyway, they hated the American Republic because it gave freedom, prosperity and the pursuit of happiness to us undeserving common folk. The Constitution gave no room for

105

evil elitists to rule, so deception is needed to destroy America from within."

"Yeah, the heart is deceptive and desperately wicked."

Patti chuckled. "You know Scripture?"

"Of course. It's our only rock of truth in this world."

Patti grinned. "Okay, I love this girl. Go ahead, Izzy."

"So, to conquer the unconquerable, the sinister plan is to gain control of the inner 'mountains' of our society. Wealthy people saw a chance to add power to their fortunes so they bought control of education, the media, entertainment, and the non-elected government. All this took decades but the final victory they hope for relies on one party political domination— then, finally, on to their dictatorship."

Emma scratched her head. "They could buy all that? But even so, why would so many surrender to them?"

"Because some feel they would share the power, others are afraid of being cancelled or having everyone think they're bad people. Going along with their plan allows some to share in the virtue signaling, but most are simply deceived by educators, politicians, and what they have heard on TV."

Patti added, "And anything you thought was good, like families and America itself, saving unborn children, asking for voters to be legal and praying in public they ridicule as evil."

"I get it, but God says 'woe to those who call evil good and good evil.' It's in Isaiah, I think."

He chuckled. "And *this* Isaiah concurs. The ones *they* think are prophets are like Saul Alinsky who said the best weapon is ridicule, but that's a weapon we can use too. We are on the front lines here, but don't think it's hopeless."

Patti tapped Emma's arm. "Right. I'm inviting you to our Youths for Freedom club. We hope to have an actual congressional candidate for a speaker this month. Say, I'll bet you also remember the quote that goes 'If He is for us, who can stand against us?'"

FAMILY

Beth came in the front door with a bag of groceries singing a tune. She followed the "Hi, Dear" greeting and found Owen reclined in his Lazy Boy, reading the newspaper.

"Well, don't you look comfortable."

Owen put down the paper and moved the chair to upright. "Did you forget I worked a night shift? I only got home at nine this morning. How did substitute teaching go?"

Beth headed for the kitchen but answered, "Oh, great. Fifth graders have such open minds. Just keep them interested and challenged and discipline is no problem."

"You read to them again, didn't you?"

She came back into the room chuckling. "Only for a half hour. If they are diligent in their course work, I reward them with a chapter. I'm reading through Kipling's, The Jungle Book."

"Really?" Owen got up and gave his wife a kiss. "I would think today's kids would only be happy with full color audio-video and surround sound."

"Not true. A good novel lets one's imagination form pictures in the mind's eye, and Kipling is brilliant." She looked up and gestured with elocutionary style. "You should have seen their faces today when I read"— Big breath. "'The great snake, Kaa, slowly slithered down the muddy bank into the river, the great, green, greasy Limpopo River.'" Her expression said, "See what I mean?"

"I admit, that's truly poetic prose. You should sign up for children's reading hour at the library."

She sighed. "They stopped that for another program."

"Oh, no, not the Drag Queen story hour?"

She nodded grimly, then looked at the clock. "It's time to meet Zoe Ann at the bus stop. Want to come?"

"Absolutely, and I have some interesting news."

In the elevator Beth asked, "Is it something about your work? A problem with the prayer time?"

"No, no. Work is fine. I got a call from the adoption agency--a conference call with another man. Remember that Zoe Ann's only living relative was an uncle in rehab?"

Half way down the front steps, Beth stopped. "If this man thinks he's going to take her away, he'll have to kill me first."

Owen laughed. "Easy, Mama Bear. No, this guy, Fredrick Smith, owns a computer repair business in Denver. He's in Chicago for a convention and just wants to meet his niece tomorrow. As her only family, how could I say no—and get this. He tells me he knows who her father is."

UNCLE FRED

The next day, Beth admitted being nervous about the sudden appearance of Zoe Ann's family member. "My head tells me there's no danger that we'll lose our child, but my insides still feel all twisted up."

"It'll be fine, darling. He seems like a nice guy and he said he couldn't stay for dinner. He has to talk at this convention of his."

They had Zoe Ann working on a Disney puzzle in the dining room so they could talk to him first. When the doorbell rang at five, Beth gave a little hop and covered her mouth. Owen squeezed her shoulders and made eye contact. "Stay cool, sweetheart. We'll answer it together."

Fred was a handsome, sandy-haired man in his forties. He wore a tweed sports jacket and a big smile greeting. "Hi. Delighted to meet you two." They shook hands. "The woman at the Center kept talking about how great a family you are."

Owen ushered him in. "A bit of an exaggeration, I think."

Beth offered him coffee, but he declined. She said, "We would have called you when Zoe Ann came to us, but they said you were, uh, indisposed."

"That's putting it kindly. I had a cocaine habit to break. I deceived myself into thinking I couldn't do software programming without it. The rehab got me drug free, but more importantly they led me to Christ."

Beth relaxed into a big grin. "Praise the Lord. Have a seat. Can I get you anything?"

"A glass of water would be nice."

While Beth left to get it, Owen said, "We'll let you meet Zoe Ann in a moment. They said you had a computer repair store?"

"Well, I started that way a long time ago. I own the Mighty Bytes store chain. Have you heard of them?"

"Yes, they are all over. I'm impressed. Are you married?"

"An almost doesn't count, does it?"

Beth returned with the water. "Please tell us about Zoe Ann's family. We'll get you two together in a sec."

"First, let me say, what a beautiful name you chose. The center told me she wouldn't be alive if it weren't for you and the clinic nurse. Thanks. I'm truly in your debt."

Owen said, "The nurse was Celia Holt. She really should get all the credit for saving Zoe Ann's life."

"Great. I hope she's doing well. My only sibling was a sister. She and her husband died in an auto accident when Ann was about twelve. Our mother was widowed and took care of her granddaughter for a few years before she passed. Ann was on her own then and pretty independent-minded. She worked as a waitress from her early teens. My only contact was her hand drawn cards at Christmas. I feel guilty I never asked if she wanted any help."

A child's voice came from the other room. "Mommy, there's a missing piece."

Beth giggled and motioned toward Fred. "Time for you to meet her independent-minded daughter."

As they entered the kitchen, Zoe Ann said, "Look, Mommy, I've only got three pieces left and none of them fit into the sky."

Ignoring that, Beth said, "Guess what, dear, here is that relative of yours I said would come by. Zoe Ann, this is your Uncle Fred."

Fred gave her a smile. "I'm delighted to meet you, Zoe Ann. I see you are as pretty as your mother."

"You knew Mother Ann?"

Beth turned to leave. "I'll let you two get acquainted."

Fred said, "Not well, but I saw her twice and we exchanged some notes."

Zoe Ann's head dropped. "Ginny's mom said I killed her."

Fred pulled a chair around and sat facing her. "Zoe Ann, that is *so* not true, and I'm sure that's not what she meant. Your mom had an unusual condition and only died because she couldn't get to a hospital. Don't you *ever* think it was your fault."

Zoe Ann thought about that for a moment then looked right at him. "Were you her brother?"

"I was her *mom's* brother so I'm actually your grand uncle, but just call me Uncle Fred, okay?"

"Okay." A little smile glimmered. "I've got some of Mommy Ann's drawings."

"Oh, I'd love to see them, but aren't you going to finish the puzzle first?"

"Can't. There's a missing piece."

Fred craned his neck and looked all around. "What's that little thing on the floor by the wall?"

Zoe Ann let out a squeak, jumped down and retrieved it. Back at the table she quickly added the remaining pieces. "There, all done. Thanks, Uncle Fred."

Fred stood to admire it. "That's 'Frozen Two,' right?"

"Yup." She grabbed his hand and led him away. "Come on. I'll show you her pictures."

They paraded through the small living room with Fred in tow. He waved at her parents. "I think she's in charge." They laughed.

Fred stood in awe as he took in all the drawings covering the walls in Zoe Ann's room. "What grade are you in, dear?"

"Third."

"Wow, you sure have you mother's talent."

Zoe Ann bounded over to the wall and touched a drawing. "A lot of them *are* Mother Ann's, silly. The ones next to hers I did a year ago, but I'm gonna redo my bad ones someday."

"All better than I could do. What have you done lately?"

"Watercolors mostly. There's one on the refrigerator and," she pointed to a framed work over her headboard. "That one I did after our trip to Lake Michigan."

Fred moved in for a closer look. "Gosh, that could be a Winslow Homer. I love the way the sailboat is turning and a girl is leaning out on the other side."

"Uh, huh. That's what they were doing when they got close to the shore, A man was shouting something, too."

Fred chuckled. "But you can't paint that, can you?"

"Can too. See his head over the sail? His mouth is open."

"You are truly amazing, Zoe Ann. When it's time for Christmas presents, I'd like a little watercolor. Was that the last one you did?"

"Last watercolor. I've been trying to learn oil paints this year. They're hard. I've painted over all the ones I did first."

Fred pointed to an easel turned away in the corner. "Is that one a painting you're working on now?"

"Yeah, but I don't want to show anybody until its finished, and it's on my only Gesso board."

"Oh, please. I'll be flying back to Denver soon."

Zoe Ann chuckled. "Oh, all right." She turned the easel around. "Maybe you can answer a question about it."

The grandeur and detail of Zoe Ann's work left Fred open-mouthed and stunned. He sat on the edge of her bed to study it. "Oh, my, I wasn't expecting this."

On the top, the loving face of God looked down and angels trumpeted from the upper corners. Below was a large circle, perhaps the Earth, but instead of land and sea, it had multiple compartments. A few were filled in with fishes at the bottom, birds at the top and small furry creatures along the sides. In an inner, center circle a man stood holding hands with a woman with the White House in the background.

Fred gestured toward the painting. "I can't believe someone you age could create this. This is how you see God's creation, isn't it? This is simply *beautiful*, Zoe Ann."

"Thanks, but some colors aren't right yet. Do you have any suggestions for the empty compartments?"

He stroked his chin. "Um, maybe a sailboat and dolphins?"

"Oooh, yes, *dolphins*. Thanks, Uncle Fred."

"I wish I didn't have to head out so soon. I'll be back, one day, but I have to go now. Everyone is going to *love* your painting." He gave her a hug and a wave good bye.

Back in the living room, Fred faced her parents. "I don't know if you realize it, but you have an actual child prodigy here. Loved meeting you, but I have to get back to the convention."

Owen said, "Not so fast. Did you think I forgot what you said about her father?"

"Oh, right, and what I've just seen totally confirms it. Ann had written me a few notes, but in one of the last ones she said, 'Oops, I have a total crush on my professor.' She was taking a night course in art."

Beth said, "Do you know who the professor was?"

"Yes, and It's amazing he would even take the time to do a guest teaching. Her professor was Sylvan Moss."

"*The* Sylvan Moss? The boy wonder on Time Magazine?"

"Yup, the same. He's about thirty five now and in Paris doing gallery tours. Remember, he did that enormous painting

117

on the building in St. Louis. It would take a DNA test to prove it, but I'm willing to bet he is Zoe Ann's father."

Owen said. "Wow—not sure what we'll do with this."

Beth gave him a look of concern. "I think, for now, it better be our family secret."

WISTERIA

They exchanged the truth of God for the lie, and
Worshiped and served the creature rather than
The Creator. Romans 1: 24, NJKV

The young man bounced out onto the small stage like he'd just won the lottery. "Hello, hello, and welcome to Youths for Freedom!" I think we have twice as many here since last month's meeting, and I know why. We are absolutely thrilled that a congressional candidate has agreed to speak to little old us."

Patti nudged Emma. "See, I told you she'd come."

The MC raised his hands. "So, without any more introduction, here is one who will fight for truth and every American citizen. Here is the one who will restore our government to the people. I present to you, our next congresswoman from District Five." Gesturing offstage, "I proudly give you Wisteria Smart!"

A black woman in a skirt and pink blouse hurried to the podium, waving, while the audience stood, cheered and applauded. "Thank you, thank you," she said with a wide grin. I only hope I can live up to those expectations."

"Manny, my campaign manager, said why go there? Half of them aren't old enough to vote, but I reminded him of the new Progressive voting rules. Since they mail ballots to every address in the country, you get to vote for your great grandfather." Laughter. "You *know* how he'd vote if he were alive, right? But, be careful, that foxy guy might be voting twice." More laughter. "See, now they've stamped out voter suppression."

Wisteria opened a folder on the podium. "This isn't going to be a campaign speech. It will be more like that lecture you won't get in college. It is obvious that America has become divided, is under attack and in trouble. Let's look at what's behind these awful developments.

"It is human nature to want to be in control of one's life. That can be a good thing if say, you are managing your own business enterprise. It is an evil thing if you seek to control everyone else for the sake of your own money and power. Unfortunately, the history of our world shows us that authoritarian regimes have been the norm—kings in the past and one-party rulers in the present. Many leaders have even claimed divinity and demanded to be worshiped.

"Communists and Fascists seem to war against each other." Wisteria chuckled. "But did you notice that they both include socialist in their titles? Kings were more intellectually honest. They just conquered a land and kept their subjects in line with their armies. Present day dictators need to deceive a population first before they're able to secure a government with force. I recall that Joseph Stalin was once asked how he could control tens of millions of people. He replied, 'Lie to them.'"

Wisteria smiled and searched the eager faces looking up at her. "The American Revolution is a beautiful thing, but it totally shook up the totalitarian world. Our born-again Christian Founders not only rebelled against a King, but against rulers controlling subjects. Our Constitution affirms everyone's God given rights, but it also establishes a Republic in which we ordinary citizens now control our own government."

She looked up for a moment with open hands, "God is *so* much a part of our American Republic. For the first time in history, we had a government recognizing our Creator and His rights, given and guaranteed to each one of us. We formed One Nation Under God." Wisteria cupped one hand behind an ear. "Listen. You can hear Satan screaming." Audience laughter.

"The atheistic, self-serving, would-be totalitarian rulers absolutely *hate* America. Their tactic to destroy us is the same as Satan's—deception and false accusations shouted with indignation as though *they* were the moral ones. That tactic is illegal both under our law and God's. Remember, thou shalt not bear false witness against your neighbor?"

"One false accusation is hilarious, though. The Elites are now accusing freedom loving Americans as being Fascists. A

121

fascist government is one that exalts a nation above the individual and is run by a dictator who uses the central government to forcibly suppress the opposition. That is so *totally* opposite of the Constitution that we love, but it is exactly what the Progressive extremists are trying to impose—a government of one party." Wisteria paused and leaned forward on the podium. "Notice how they always accuse us of what *they* are doing. We're supposed to be haters, but they hate us truth-talkers big time."

Patti nudged Emma. "There—just what I told you."

"A hundred years ago, Communists complained about unfair labor practices as their rallying cry and overthrew a government. As we now know, their new government established *horribly* unfair labor practices. But today, what trick are like-minded autocrats going to use to destroy a happy Christian country with a prosperous middle class earning good wages? I can imagine them meeting in some multimillion-dollar home, swirling brandy and smoking cigars. 'I know,' one said, 'Forget that slavery ended a hundred and fifty years ago. We'll stop teaching history and teach deceptive propaganda starting in kindergarten. From now on the United States will be described as a hotbed of racial persecution and we will take over as their savior.' These autocrats spent billions in the hope that their deceptions would destroy our Constitutional Republic and they, the Elite, would rule again."

Wisteria stepped to one side and pretended to wipe her brow. Deep breath. "Do not be fooled into thinking that this latest tactic is where the Progressives began. They just ramped up their hysterical rhetoric when a constitution-loving president was elected. Anyone of *any* race who disagrees with their neo-Marxist agenda is cancelled and called racist, fascist, bigot, white supremacist and perhaps even a domestic terrorist. We ignorant deplorables *must be* ruled for our own good. Cancellation might be the current term for this, but I call it Social Terrorism.

"You should understand that the Progressive Elites have been at work on their 'Destroy America Plan' for a hundred years. With nearly unlimited finances they now dominate what is known as the mountains of society. They have a controlling influence on Education, the Media, Entertainment, big business, the inner non-elected government, and they want to secularize religion and destroy the family. Next, they hope to institute a one-party system and take full control of your country along with your freedom, peace property and your prosperity. And you must realize this: they, like Satan, will be *utterly* ruthless in reaching their goal.

"In conclusion, we are faced with a powerful menace. Should we surrender?" The audience shouted a chorus of "No's."

"But they will spew curses and accusations on you. They will put some of you in prison to scare the rest of you. They will claim that everything you thought you owned and even your children belong to the *State*. Your protests will be met by government police. What weapons do we have?" Silence, mumbling. "First, we still have our votes if we can get the system honest again, but our best weapon is faith--faith that God is with us and that *His* truth will prevail."

The youthful audience erupted into cheers, applause and a USA chant. Wisteria blew them a kiss as she waved and walked out.

LITTLE LOST ONE

The driver, Mike, Owen and his friend, Jim, left the hospital parking lot heading back to base. Mike turned into the street and accelerated with a roar. "That was the third heart attack we had this week. You'd think it was contagious."

Owen said, "At least this last one had the decency to have his at nine in the morning. I almost finished my breakfast."

Jim chuckled. "Wait, are you about to suggest our next stop should be for an Egg McMuffin?"

"No need." He picked up a brown bag. "We've got our lunches. I am thinking about a lower fat diet though, and— woah, wait. Mike, pull over, won't you?"

"Sure, what's up?"

"You guys, stay put." He opened his lunch bag, pulled out a piece of ham from a sandwich and opened the door. "Jim, google the nearest Humane Society, won't you?"

They watched as Owen walked back half a block, then sat down on the sidewalk, squatting down against a building. He was calling out and dangling the ham. When there were no passers-by, a dark brown Dachshund hesitatingly came out from under a car and moved toward him.

It took a few minutes of coaxing and tossing bits of meat, but finally the dog was in his arms. Back in the van, their canine friend became relaxed, friendly and curious about all their lunch bags. With Jim's phone directions, they headed for the Animal Shelter. "That was nice of you, Owen, but we're just gonna drop him off, right?"

"Her. We have a little lady." The little lady had found Owen's lap and was bestowing kisses. "Hopefully, we can find the owner. Her collar has no address."

Mike said, "Better just drop her off. We don't have all morning."

As they pulled into the Shelter, Owen reassured them. "I'll know one way or another in a few moments." He got out holding the dog under one arm like a football and turned back to his friends. He waved the dog's paw at them, "Back soon."

Ten minutes later, after only one impatient toot of the horn, Owen reappeared with the dachshund on a leash. After she did a squat on the lawn, he picked her up and got back in the van. "Her name's Digger and she lives at 124 Oak Avenue."

Jim pecked at his phone and mumbled. "And, how in the heck did you find that out?"

"Good dog owners put in ID chips."

Mike said, "Really? Maybe dementia patients should get one too."

Jim said, "Got the address. It's just a mile away in the burbs. Turn left on ninth."

In a few minutes they were pulling into the circular drive of a private home. Owen hastened to the doorbell.

The woman who answered let out a shriek of delight and scooped up her wiggly canine. "Oh, thank you, *thank you* so much, mister." She called back into her house. "Ronny, come quick. See who's at the door."

She shook her head. "This bad dog dug under the fence. We posted a five-hundred-dollar reward. Can I write you a check?"

"Oh, no Ma'am, I..."

Eight-year-old Ronny came running up and he and Digger were soon kissing and flailing over the hall rug in a delirious reunion.

Mother and Owen laughed with delight. He said, "No, Ma'am, I just got a better reward."

CHOICES

Time has passed, and it was now nearing the end of Isaiah's junior year. Beth and Owen sat on a park bench enjoying a pleasant spring day while they watched Zoe Ann at play with her friends. Owen put his elbow over the back rest and turned to his wife. "I don't get it. I'm finally able to afford sending our genius son to a better college and he says 'no thanks.' Every vacation we hear about his being tortured by the 'wokeistas' and this would be a perfect escape for him."

Beth nodded. "And better education opportunities too, but there's two reasons."

"Really. What have I missed?"

"The first one is obvious. He's involved with that Freedom Youth group and their cause to champion liberty and truth on campus. He's very excited about their mission and he feels needed there."

"True, but I don't buy that as a reason to turn down a good education opportunity. Besides, they must have chapters on most colleges. What's the second reason?"

"The second reason is what you saw when he was here on his spring break last week, and last Christmas. That reason is about five foot five, with fluffy blonde hair and a mind as sharp as our son's."

"Oh, phss." Owen chuckled. "He's in *college,* Beth. Hanging out with girls is what we guys do, Hon."

Beth patted his arm. "We women have a perception that most men don't have. Isaiah told me he thinks God sent Patti to him."

"Nah look, he came back that night after their day at the beach. Nothing happened. He's a good kid."

"Owen, I had time for a chat with Patti while you two were shooting balls into your golf net."

He pointed at her. "But we *also* did a delicate computer repair and virus removal. Anyway, he did tell me he liked the girl. So what?"

Beth sighed and bestowed a look of sympathy on him. "Listen, darling. Isaiah and Patti are deeply in love—a profound, Holy Spirit anointed, forever love."

His back stiffened. "Woah, you could tell *that* from just one meeting?"

Big smile. "Oh yes. Feminine intuition, not to mention a mother's perception. It was a delight to behold."

"So, you think they'll get married? They're not engaged."

"Isaiah is spending two days at her parents in July. My guess is he'll propose to her then."

A finger went up. "He sold that gold coin from my father—said it was for an investment. Why wouldn't he tell me if it was for a ring?"

"Because he thinks she might say no, and she might even think of reasons to say no to marriage at this time, but a love *that* powerful will bowl them over like ten pins. She'll say yes."

Owen laughed. "Feminine intuition is impressive. I hope you're right, but we'll just have to wait and—oops there goes my phone."

Beth got up. "Okay, you talk. Zoe Ann wants a swing push."

The phone ID said "Illinois Correction Facility." Owen was puzzled but decided to answer.

Is this Owen Wilson? This is Celia Holt. They'll only give me one call so please don't hang up.

REVENGE

Owen took a few steps and turned away from the playground noise. "Celia, what's going on? We haven't heard from you in years."

I've been in Denver—got my nursing degree. Look, the Unplanned Mothers Clinic must have figured out I saved that infant. The police pounded on my door at six AM, put me in handcuffs and arrested me. They claim I stole clinic supplies. Never happened.

"Course you didn't, and that was years ago. Are you in Illinois now?"

Yeah, they said I'm a fugitive from justice, put me on a smelly bus and extradited me back here. All my stuff is in Denver and I don't have a lawyer. This jail is just awful—I...(crying)

"Oh, this is terrible, Celia, but don't you worry. We'll think of something. Maybe I can visit you tomorrow."

God, I hope so but they said lawyers only. I don't know what to (sob) *do. Uh, oh, they're gonna take the phone away. Time's up.*

"Lets both pray. You'll hear from..." Click.

Beth came back with Zoe Ann and he caught her up on the event. They headed back to their apartment with Beth mumbling under her breath. "That clinic is just horrid." Suddenly, she stopped. "Hey. I know who to call. Uncle Fred is in town again and he must know more than we do about lawyers.

And, Uncle Fred did. He was incensed about it and told them, "Celia is the woman who saved Zoe Ann's life. I'm all in. I'll be there with counsel tomorrow."

*   *   *

The next morning Fred arrived at the jail with criminal attorney Kristin Newman. She worked for the law firm used by Mighty Bytes: Schindler, Fitton and Foster.

They found Celia in a jail cell shared with another woman. She was squeezed into a corner on a cot, hugging her knees. Contorted with fear, she looked up at them. The attorney approached her with a smile and extended her hand. "Miss Holt, I am Kristin Newman and I will be your attorney if you agree. We can move to a consultation room."

Celia shook her hand. "That would be great, but I don't have much money."

In the private room, Kristin continued, "Let me introduce Fredrick Smith. He is the grand uncle of the child you rescued and has agreed to pay all of your expenses."

Celia gave him a smile. "Wow, thank you, Sir."

Fred returned it. "Call me Fred. It's my pleasure and my honor to meet you, Celia. You risked a lot to save that infant's life and Zoe Ann is my only living relative."

Kristin removed a folder from her briefcase. "Our firm has already done a preliminary investigation. Celia, anything you say to me is covered by attorney-client privilege and will not be shared. I understand that you saved this child from the abortion center with the help of emergency medical services, correct?"

"Yes Ma'am."

"Just Kristin is fine." She gave a reassuring smile and a nod. "I also assume you did not steal anything from the clinic."

"Not a thing, and I quit because it was too horrible to work there. They sell the baby parts, you know."

"Yuck." Kristin stuck out her tongue and shook her head. "But I understand they kill the baby by puncturing the skull as the child is being born. Why didn't the doctor do that?"

Celia let out a big breath. "Two reasons, I think. The placenta was in the way and there was massive bleeding. The baby came out feet first. The doctor had the instrument in his hand but stopped."

"Do you know why?"

"I think—I think because Zoe Ann opened her eyes and looked at him. Instead, he just tossed her onto a roll cart."

"Don't make your lawyer cry. There was a second reason?"

"Yeah. Ann, the mother, was having a seizure. The nurse was bag breathing her and he shot something into her IV, but she died anyway. That's when he said for me to call the ambulance, and he and the nurse left."

Kristin leaned back in her chair. "Left? All right, that fills in some blanks. My presumption is that the clinic was taking revenge on you for denying them the sale of the body parts, but why would they wait so many years?"

"I kept talking with a friend of mine at the clinic. She said they first assumed it was the maid, Maria Gonzales, who saved the baby--you know, being Catholic and all. They fired her and put her in jail for theft."

"Then why go after you?"

"A Latino Justice Foundation got her case reopened after two years and cleared her. I had erased the surveillance video of my letting the EMT man, uh, I mean Owen, out the back door, but maybe they had a backup. A new administrator came on, and when another nurse made an attempt to save a baby, I think they wanted to scare others out of trying. Also, it must have taken time to find me in Denver."

Kristin shook her head. "Well, they sure are vicious, but I think we can make them pay. First, you will be released on bail thanks to your benefactor here. Next, the Wilsons want you to stay with them."

"Oh, cool. I get to see Zoe Ann, too?"

"I thought you'd like that." Kristin grinned.

Fred waved his hand. "Just *wait* till you see her. She's a child prodigy and an amazing kid."

Kristin continued. "Here is our legal strategy. I'm sure the clinic will drop the case after a little negotiation. We'll let them know that we'll charge *them* for bringing false and malicious charges, not to mention medical malpractice, and negligent homicide relating to the mother. I doubt the clinic will want the cost and publicity. Any questions?"

Celia grinned and shook her head. "Wow, thanks." She turned to Fred. "You know, it might take me years to pay you back."

He chuckled. "No need, and I seriously doubt you are a flight risk."

Kristin stood up. "All right then. Time for me to get to work, but first, let's get you out of this creepy place."

SCHOOL DAZE

A few more years have passed. Zoe Ann is now in fifth grade and her artwork has been displayed at two state fairs and even one prestigious gallery. Isaiah and Patti are married—no surprise, and they live a few blocks from his parents. He is developing new cyber security software for Mighty Bytes who hired him despite condemnation letters from his faculty. Patti works as a teacher in a Charter school. Before Isaiah graduated, he was once on television after being badly beaten by a BLM protest mob. He was trying to get statements and record their interviews.

Celia was not only cleared of the charges, she was awarded fifty thousand dollars in a non-disclosure settlement. She moved back to Illinois and now works as a hospital nurse, near enough to the Wilsons to be a regular babysitter for Zoe Ann. Today she is returning from the bus stop with her charge.

"Honey, tell your mom about what you heard in school today. I want to know more about it myself."

Beth gave her daughter a welcome embrace. "Come on into the kitchen, you two. Whatever it is, Zoe Ann is more talkative with milk and cookies going in—oh, wait, now it's grown-up granola bars, right?"

Zoe Ann was well along in her transformation toward womanhood. She had coifed her hair into one braid running down her back and her pink fingernails bore tiny flowers, each of her own design. She placed her backpack beside the kitchen chair and slipped off mother Ann's hand-embroidered jeans jacket. Gracefully slipping into the chair, she grinned. "Thanks, Mom. Can I show you a sketch I made first?"

"Of course. We just love your work, Darling."

Zoe Ann pulled out her sketchbook from the backpack. "I did this in class. I think Miss Walsh thought I was taking notes while she taught history."

Beth said, "Well, I hope you didn't miss out on the lesson."

"Oh, Mother—course not. I know all the reasons for the American Revolution. Isaiah's pop quizzes, remember?"

She flipped to the page and turned it toward the women. Celia gasped, took hold of it and sat down in a chair. "Good, *Lord*, girl, this is absolutely fantastic."

The pencil drawing showed a woman in three quarter view in exquisite detail, her expression conveying love and concern. "It's Miss Walsh. She's so pretty."

Celia chuckled. "Sure beats giving teacher an apple."

"Nope." Zoe Ann took a grand bite of granola bar. "I can't show it to her now—I'll wait until the end of the school year. Say, I thought Daddy would be home by now."

Beth pulled the sketch over to look more closely. "Yes, but sometimes they get a call just before the shift change. Funny he hasn't called me, though. What did you hear today?"

"Oh, right. It was about Johnny Cook. I don't know him real well cause he's in eighth grade." She pointed to the fruit bowl on the center of the table. "Can I have one of those little oranges?"

"Sure Honey. They're mandarins."

Zoe Ann took the fruit and began to peel it thoughtfully. "We all knew what happened to him 'cause his parents were in the hall shouting at the principal about parent's rights. The principal called them transphobic and other stuff."

"Johnny did something wrong?"

"No, no—see, Johnny wanted to be Jennifer all this year after those secret counseling sessions he had. He, er, *she* dresses like a girl and we've been nice to her. Parents aren't allowed to attend the meetings—'confidential' they say. There has been a lot of talk about that. I told you before, remember?"

"Oh, yes, and I talked to his mom at a school board meeting. It's all so wrong. So, they were angry about that, huh?"

"Oh, yeah. Johnny, uh Jennifer went to a hospital somewhere to have girl surgery. His parents weren't told and the principal wouldn't tell them where he was."

Celia's head crashed onto her arms on the table and Beth jumped up. "Oh, Lord forbid! *No*! They *can't* do that without parents knowing, can they?"

"Yeah, it's something about new government rules. They say they're protected by confidentiality and call the surgery gender affirming. Psychologists and the HEW know more about children than parents, they say. They know better cause we're not educated."

Beth paced around the kitchen for a few minutes, her foot slapping the floor as she turned. No one said anything. Finally, she sat, let out a big breath and took their hands in hers. "Time to pray."

"Pray for Jennifer, Mom?"

"Yes, and we must pray that this deceiving evil will be cast out from among us."

QUESTIONS

Owen grimaced while his son implored him on the phone. "Come on, Dad, it'll be fun. It's the last debate before the election, and the Republican candidate for our district is only behind by four points."

"This district has been Democrat for fifty years, and besides, I'm into a good novel."

Isaiah laughed. "Now, if you had said 'golf,' I might believe you. Look, you can read at bedtime. Patti and I think this could be historic. They're doing a Town Hall at one tomorrow afternoon, and *we* get to ask them questions."

"Okay, but you know I tend to shout when I hear lies."

Laughing again, "I'm counting on it. Besides, I already registered you for a question."

*   *   *

The moderator, an attractive Asian woman in a yellow print dress, reviewed the rules and presented the candidates. The six-term incumbent, Charles Simpkins, spent most of his dissertation claiming that only he could bring about unity, peace, prosperity and equity. Although he was gray-haired and white, his fiery conclusion claimed his opponent, a middle-aged black woman named Wisteria Smart, would try and suppress minority votes and was a fascist tool of white supremacy.

Wisteria began her concluding rebuttal after a moment of head nodding. She faced the audience with a wide grin. "Wow, what zingers. I never realized I was the 'black face of white supremacy.' That's quite an accomplishment for the great, great granddaughter of a Georgia slave," They laughed. "And freed by the Republicans, I might add."

"Also, if I'm supposed to be doing the bidding of bad white guys, I could have used their help getting me through law school." Pause. "My opponent's accusation is actually quite racist and it reveals his true colors. The neo-Marxist left does not even consider that we blacks can, or should, think for ourselves. They are shocked to discover that we like to earn a good living, own a home and even a business. How *dare* a black woman deny being oppressed and rebel against their totalitarian demands." Pause. She glanced at Simpkins who looked like he had indigestion.

"They would like us to believe there has been no progress toward equality in this country and only a benevolent, all-knowing government can save us from oppression. They would deny us a good education, destroy the strength of our families, remove police protection and still expect our grateful votes to keep them in power. We Blacks have now become *their* deceived voting slaves—or so they hope."

Simpkins shouted. "Outrageous lies!"

Ms. Smart took another head-nodding pause. "Let's look at Simpkins final accusation—that I am guilty of spreading 'the big lie' about voter fraud in our last presidential election. I contend that the only big lie is that it was an honest election. We don't have time to go into each of the many incidents and sworn testimonies here, but go to my website for details."

Simpkins shouted, "No credible evidence!"

Ms. Smart gave a brief speech about her ideas to restore the economy, bring back energy independence, take action to secure our boarder, reinvigorate the military and police, and insure children are educated, not force-fed Marxist propaganda. While there were a few boos, the audience applauded loudly.

The moderator stepped forward. "All right, all right. I think we are now ready for our voter questions. First, those who have registered in advance." He looked at his cards. "Is Mister Owen Wilson here?"

Owen stood up and accepted the microphone. "Yes, I am he. That exchange just changed what I was going to ask. Mister Simpkins: the grandson of John Rockefeller owns the largest of our Social Media sites. Do you think the 400 million he spent on the big city precincts of swing states, with his cash dependent on following his direction, had any effect on the 2020 election?"

"Not at all. The money just helped people vote in the time of the pandemic."

"So, you think local, state and federal laws had to be violated in order for people to vote?"

"This was a pandemic emerg..." He slammed his palm on the podium and pointed at Owen. "*You!* You're the one arrested for disrupting a school board meeting, aren't you?"

"I wasn't arrested. I *was* indignant, though. They are teaching obscene things to our children."

Simpkins looked at the moderator, still pointing at Owen. "I'm not taking any more questions from that bigot."

Wisteria had her hand up and the moderator gestured to her. "Would you like to comment on voting, Ms. Smart?"

"Rather than diving into details here, I note that several states have now passed laws prohibiting 'contributions' directly to those working in voting precincts. I refer our listeners to the DVD titled 'Rigged' produced by Citizens United."

"A Nazi organization. Don't buy it," shouted Simpkins.

The moderator grinned. She checked her cards and looked around at the audience. "All righty, then. Let's get the next question from a woman." She chuckled. "No offense intended toward anyone not liking that designation. Uh, Patricia, you're next."

Patti stood up with a grin and a little wave. "Mister Simpkins, it became well known, especially after the contents of a famous laptop was revealed, that the president's family was involved with taking money from China, Russia, Ukraine and doing them favors. The New York Post was cancelled by social media at the demand of the FBI for revealing this. Many Democrats stated they would have changed their vote if these facts were made public. Don't you think this may have swung the election?"

"They *aren't* facts, and why are we discussing a past presidential election anyway? Next question."

Wisteria didn't raise her hand, so the moderator looked at her card. "All right, Bridgit O'Malley."

A middle-aged woman with red hair and a bright green dress took the microphone. "To answer *your* question, Sir, we are asking about that election because the FBI lied about the laptop and forced censorship on the media. Meanwhile, *your* party accused everybody else of the 'big lie.' Look, we common folk just want to know our elections are honest."

Bridgit let out a big breath. "Okay, my question is this: with over 400 sworn testimonies of fraud, videos of under the table ballots coming out at night, ballot stuffing and a truck driver describing a semi rig full of ballots going from Long Island to Pennsylvania, why were there no court trials?"

"There were, and the judges found the evidence had no merit. Next question."

This time Wisteria's hand was up. She said, "The judges were too afraid to hold trials so they refused the cases and never heard the testimonies given under oath or saw the videos. Another documentary to watch is '2000 Mules.'"

Moderator: "Next, we have a voter with a biblical name. Is Isaiah here?"

Isaiah grinned as he took the microphone. "Aren't we glad we cleared all that up?" The audience laughed. "It's no laughing matter that almost everyone associated with the previous administration is either under subpoena or indicted when they speak the truth. Politics has always been a blood sport, but now we are verging on a police state. I would just add that some judges and state AGs ignored or illegally changed the election laws at the last minute. Also, countrywide, 92 million completely unsecure mail-in ballots were sent out."

Simpkins shouted at the moderator. "What is this? You only registered people from the Fascist Youth Corps?"

The moderator called out, "Isaiah, you're in college and registered as an Independent, right?"

"Yup."

"Do you have a *question*?"

"Sure. Mister Simpkins, how do you justify your parties' deliberate actions to let in two million foreigners per year including girls for human trafficking, and make little effort to stop Fentanyl which has killed a hundred thousand young

145

people this year. Also, why did you recklessly put our country into debt we cannot repay, hire 81,000 new IRS agents who must carry weapons of war, and mandate the teaching of Pornography and Marxism in our grade schools?"

Simpkins waved him off with the back of his hand. "All those are lies straight out of right-wing propaganda. They are explained and debunked on my Simpkins for Congress web site."

The moderator gestured toward Wisteria who was laughing. "Isaiah, when you finish college, I think you should run for Congress—in another district, of course." Audience laughter.

With a sweeping point to the back of the room the moderator said, "We have time for one more question from the audience. This lady has been waving the whole time."

The mike came to a heavy-set black woman. "Bonnie Sears, here. I'm a registered Democrat, but I'm gonna rethink that idea. Whoever names your new laws is clever, though. Affordable Care---nope, Infrastructure Act—hardly, Inflation Reduction—nope, and the Defense of Marriage Act—actually an attack on true marriage and people of faith. Best of all though, is your calling true statements the 'big lie.' My question: do you think historians are gonna call what *you all* are doing 'The Great Deception'?"

Simpkins slammed his folder shut and pointed at the moderator. "We're done here. You engineered this as a political hit piece, didn't you? Your network will be hearing from us."

FLASHBACK

We should no longer be children tossed to and fro
And carried about with every wind of doctrine by
The trickery of men and deceitful plotting. Eph. 4:14

CHINESE EMBASY, WASHINGTON DC, July 2017

Sylvia Watkins, Deputy Director of the NIH ushered into the office of the Chinese science advisor, Xi Fang, smiling as they shook hands. "This will be a most sensitive discussion, Mister Fang. Do you have the area secured?"

He chuckled. "Far better than you Americans do, but shall we go to the reception lounge?" He gestured to the adjoining room. "Care for some tea?"

The lounge boasted full Chinese elegance with a waitress standing at attention. They sat opposite each other with an antique low table between them. The ornately carved chairs arms ended with angry "Temple Dogs," but welcomed them with plush embroidered pillows. The waitress poured their teas and was dismissed. Fang opened up his hands. "How can we be of service to your most generous NIH?"

"Doctor Fungo believes it is time for an experimental trial of our gain of function virus."

A wide-eyed stare. "*Does* he, now." A sip of tea. "Our team is proud of Operation Cobra Strike, but we are still working on problems. The good news is that our venom-tipped spike proteins attack blood vessels, lungs and the heart, but we are concerned that Corona viruses are too easily treated. Recently, our bio-weapons lab has been re-exploring the weaponizing of smallpox instead."

Sylvia lifted her teacup from the table and felt for a moment that the carved dragons on its corners looked up and growled at her. "I, uh, don't you remember? Doctor Fungo said, and you agreed, that testing gain of function research would be more important than the pandemic it will cause? Besides, releasing the extinct smallpox would make your country undeniably liable."

Fang leaned back in his chair and tilted his head to one side as he considered his response. "All right, but why the *now*, Ms. Watkins?"

"Simply because it is for our mutual advantage. Our progressive march toward complete control of America was dealt an unexpected blow in our last election, and your country has suffered for it as well."

Fang nodded and he stroked his chin. "Agreed, so what do you plan to do about this setback?"

Sylvia grinned. "Plenty. Four more years of American prosperity could destroy us. Besides trying this upstart president on our made-up impeachment charges, we are using our media to make him into a pariah. Also, we are teaching our youth that the MAGAs are extremist, white supremacist Nazis."

Fang grinned. "Well done—and don't forget racist as well." They laughed. "We do hope you appreciate our helping you with the Confucius Clubs."

"Oh, yes, and we have promoted violent protests and taken legal action as well. Still, that may not be enough, but if there is a pandemic. and we can turn the people's happiness into despair, our success will be assured. Besides that, we can use the pandemic to change election laws in our favor. We also have other election fixes in mind, but without the help of a pandemic, they might not be enough. Failure is not an option. A crisis is needed to assume power over these people."

"I'm impressed, but in your country, some will speak out about what you're doing."

"Some will, but our mainstream media ridicules and demonized all those truth-speakers. We can pull licenses, and any big players will be investigated and charged by the DOJ."

Fang chuckled. "Inefficient. Here, they just disappear."

Sylvia laughed. "We're not there quite yet. Look, without a pandemic, we might not rid ourselves of this overly popular, America-loving president. That's why I'm here."

"I see." Fang took a thoughtful sip of tea. "But, before I authorize something that will kill a few million and perhaps myself, I assume you have a plan?"

"Of course. First you will not release the virus for about a year. That will give you time to make a standard vaccine in small quantities to protect yourself and those in power, including us, of course. Also, you will be richly rewarded."

"Good, but we still have to find a fix for our problem."

"Really? I'm not aware of anything major."

"There are several safe and effective antivirals out there which could stop our pandemic in its tracks. I'm speaking of hydroxychloroquine, ivermectin, fluvoxamine and the like."

Sylvia shrugged. "We will make these unavailable."

"What?" Fang sat up straight. "Those drugs are in use right now and are backed by scientific papers. Doctors will complain, not to mention everyone else."

"Our team will produce a fraudulent study to make them seem ineffective for the corona virus and the FDA will ban their use. We will remove the licenses of the first doctors who do not comply and the rest will fall in line. We are in debt to our pharmaceutical companies who have been toying with experimental RNA immunization—really just gene therapy. Fortunately, it won't prevent viral spread, but they will profit hugely, and so will we, especially when it is the only treatment allowed."

"They can also make new antivirals."

"True, and you and I will have them, but they'll only be released to the public *after* the election. By then we'll both have all the data we need on weaponized world-wide viruses."

"Excellent, but I have one more concern. I have read that RNA vaccine trials have shown many side effects. This will be especially true if your companies make them with our spike protein and its enzymes derived from cobra venom."

Sylvia shrugged. "Maybe, but none of these flaws will be reported in the mainstream press and we will cancel anyone reporting those effects from the literature of other countries. Everyone will have to accept RNA vaccines as their only hope."

Nodding his head, Fang said, "Your deceptions rival the best we have. Congratulations. I will present your plan to those who will make the final decision."

Sylvia raised a fist. "Remember: for the Greater Good!"

Fang's fist shot skyward. "For the Greater Good!"

ONWARD

The wicked prowl on every side,
When vileness is exalted among the
Sons of men. Psalm 12: 8

MARTHA'S VINYARD, JUNE 2022

The elite world movers sat on the soft chairs of a back patio overlooking an elegant garden. (Names withheld)

A man wearing shorts and a colorful Hawaiian shirt stood up. "Welcome all of you. Enough small talk--time to talk business. First, I want to reassure everyone that there are no electronics here and the perimeter is secure. Feel free to pour yourself more wine because our server will not return."

"Before we get to questions, I want to begin by reviewing what your hard-earned billions have accomplished so far. Our opposition calls it the 'plandemic,' so perhaps they realize more than we thought. However, the Chinese virus has given us all we hoped for. We were able to easily manipulate the election in favor of our puppet president with over ninety million ballots mailed out and a beautiful computer algorithm that adjusted the needed votes. We were able to magnify the January 6 protests with FBI instigators, planted 'bombs,' and a cooperative media. Also, we have frightened dissenters by jailing hundreds." Applause.

"The complete control of the population with emergency powers left us quite joyful for a while, but we need to be patient before our power becomes absolute."

"As you know from our conference at Davos, America must be destroyed before we can--" he chuckled. "Build Back Better. Yes, the Democratic party is fully ours now—or effectively so." He got up, popped a canape in his mouth and refilled his glass. Gesturing toward the gathering, he said, "There's also port and brandy here if anyone prefers."

He picked up his glass, took a sip and sighed. "The destruction process is well along and the Middle Class will effectively disappear. We will take away natural gas to heat their homes and eventually their cars and houses. Even a loss in Congress won't stop us. Thirty plus trillion in debt and continued spending will crash the economy soon and we will convert to electronic currency. We have demoralized the police and the military so their forces are weakening. Guess they'd rather retire than get 'gender training' and be sued for doing their job." (laughter) "People will have to look to the State for protection and we will respond by giving them a Federal Police Force."

"We are on track to bring in more than ten million foreigners since the start of this administration, and many are criminals who will not be jailed or deported for their activity. With the help of the cartels and the Chinese, we are expanding the euthanization of American youth. A hundred thousand are killed by fentanyl each year so they won't be serving in the military or the police. Once in control, we will form a military that serves us."

A hand flashed up, index finger skyward. "I have a concern." A slender man with slicked back hair took a puff on his cigar. "I don't think we can trust the Chinese. With our weakened defenses, why wouldn't they take over our operation?"

"A good question, but there are several reasons why they won't. First, they will be very busy acquiring control of the Asian continent, and possibly Africa as well. Likewise, our plan is to make one country out of North America and Europe. China needs a huge infusion of capital since part of their conquest will be by military force. We have supplied that in part by ordinary goods, but we have promised them that our future energy will come from the batteries, wind turbines and solar panels they supply. They need us for infusion of capital. Oh, and by facilitating nuclear weapons for Iran, they should be able to join Turkey and consolidate the region into one Islamic state."

Murmuring spread in the audience. He waved them down. "Look, when there are only two or three superpowers in the world, why would any of them want to risk everything and try to conquer the other?"

A portly, balding man spoke into his swirling brandy goblet. "The Chinese won't have that windfall if enough people realize that man-made global warming is something we made up. Comedians outside the western world are getting hysterical laughter when they poke fun at our fake climate religion."

The moderator chuckled. "True, but we should be able to gaslight them for a few more years until we have established our one-party state and nationalized all energy production. At that juncture, we will resume full use of our fossil fuels just like China does now. China will have new capital inflow from their conquests, and I expect our New World Order will receive as much revenue from fuel sales as we get from taxes." Smiles and nodding heads all around.

The first questioner pointed. "One other thing. Why should we risk parental anger with our propaganda in schools?"

"Because training our children is absolutely *fundamental* to achieve our complete victory. The nuclear family and faith are the foundation of *their* cause so these must be dismantled. The youth of our new State must be taught from preschool to reject, no make that *despise*, the God and morals of their parents. They will have no hope except for what government gives them. The history of America and Israel is now being rewritten to make them seem despicable."

He pointed back at the questioner. "Teachers, professors and after school Satan Clubs will help us achieve that purpose. With proper training, children will grow up trusting and obeying the leaders of our New World Order. We will be their new god. We don't want subjects who will just vote for us. We must have subjects willing to *die* for us." Applause.

CAMPAIGN

Wisteria's campaign headquarters occupied a vacant strip mall store. Emma stood beside Darlene, the campaign manager, who sat at her desk tapping on her phone. She was a young black woman whose attitude always defied adversity with hope.

"Darlene," Emma tossed her hands up in frustration. "We have forty-seven new college student volunteers working the streets since the Wisteria's talk, but the Dems are killing us. They have scorching TV ads—full of lies, of course—going non-stop all day. Where's all their cash coming from?"

"From George Soros and his friends, sweetheart. Listen, we are so grateful for the work all of you are putting in, and I see why you came with Patti's highest recommendation. We can only afford a tenth of their TV time, but with you guys, we have more boots on the ground, so thanks."

Emma spun on her heel and stamped her foot. "What bothers me even more than the TV, is those *disgusting* posters all over our district. How many are there, two thousand?"

"We estimate closer to three."

Emma tossed her head up. "Wow. Look, I'm studying graphic design in college. If I create a poster to counter theirs, do you think you could afford to print at least a thousand copies?"

"Oh, Emma, that's a *great* idea. We only have yard signs right now. I'm sure we could get a couple thousand. I'll speak to our treasurer. With only two months before early voting, everything helps. I can hardly wait to see your design."

*   *   *

The Simpkins poster headlined, "SAVE OUR DEMOCRACY." Under that it said, "VOTE SIMPKINS." It pictured a trousered leg, with a shoe crushing the words "MEGA MAGA" at the bottom. Down along the side a column of words read: "Stamp out: Fascism, Hate, Bigotry, White Supremacy, Misogyny, Homophobia and Domestic Terrorism."

Emma designed her poster to mimic the same visual effect. The top banner read: "DON'T LET FASCISIM CRUSH OUR REPUBLIC." The subtitle: "Guess who hates free people." The photo showed a shiny black Nazi boot complete with swastika crushing a red banner that read: "Make America Great." However, the faces of agonized men and women cried out under the boot heel as well. The side words headlined: NO MORE. Below that: STATE POWER over people, DECEPTION over truth, INDOCTRINATION over education, LAWLESSNESS over safety, OBEDIENCE over freedom, RACIST LIES over equality, CONFISCATION over rights, The ELITE over YOU."

Emma's bottom line: "Vote for AMERICA: VOTE SMART."

Wisteria's campaign raised as much money as they could and placed their posters beside Simpkins at select sites. The people would decide on whether to keep their Republic.

*   *   *

Two weeks later, Emma was driving back from campaign headquarters to her dorm, admiring her newly placed posters, at least the ones not yet torn down. Traffic halted for a light and she found herself beside a mostly empty parking lot. The two posters were plastered beside each other on a building near the sidewalk.

A young man had backed his car in and he sat on the trunk, looking at the artwork and taking pictures with his phone. That was too much to resist. Emma pulled in, backed next to him and sat on her trunk where she could study him—a handsome white guy with black scruffy hair, sporting a college hoodie.

He pretended not to notice as he tapped on his phone. Emma said, "Come here often?"

He gave a snort-laugh, looked at her and replied. "You're a student too, huh? What's your name?"

"Right. I'm Emma. Whatcha doing?"

"You can get ten bucks for every Smart poster you bring in, but dibbs on this one. Name's Sam, sweetie."

"Hi, Sam Sweetie." That got a big laugh. "So, why didn't you just grab this one and run?"

"Had to finish my burger, but I got to thinking about the message. Smart's really smashes Simpkins, don't you think?"

Emma crossed her legs, leaned toward Sam and spoke in a girly voice. "Do you think the Smart poster makes the point about who's really the fascist?"

"Oh, big time. No wonder he's paying to tear them down. These could cost him the election. Smart has a brilliant designer."

"Thank you."

"Thank you? You're helping Smart's campaign?"

"Yup. I designed this poster for her. Glad you like it."

"I'm impressed—uh," he hopped down and retrieved a black garbage bag from his car. "Now I'm feeling bad I took these two down. Want them back?"

Emma slipped off the car, peered into the bag and giggled. "Uh, uh, too wrinkled. You cash in on them."

"Nah, I quit, but maybe you could autograph one for me?"

Emma spread one out on the trunk lid, smoothing out the wrinkles and signed it with the marker he handed her. She smiled. "But, you ruined my work, so now you owe me."

"Ahh, you're right." He scratched his head. "Dinner, Friday night cover it?"

"Hmm." Head tilt and a squinty eyed look. "Maybe, but only if you stop by the barber first."

MISS WALSH

Zoe Ann's fifth grade teacher walked into her classroom wearing a tidy blue dress with yellow daisies on the fringe. She gave her students a big smile and wrote, "Ms. Walsh." On the blackboard and turned back to them. "Good morning, class. I'll start today with a word about titles and pronouns." Who remembers the title I always used before?"

Hands went up and she pointed to one. "Miss Walsh."

"Right, and who can tell us the difference?" She pointed to a girl who had a puzzled look.

"Uh—you got married?"

"Wrong. Anyone?" Zoe Ann's hand waved. "Yes?"

"It means I'm a woman and it's none of your business if I'm married or not."

She laughed. "That's such a colorful way of putting it, Zoe Ann, but yes, it is neutral regarding marital status, just like Mr. is for Mister. If men don't have to reveal their status, then neither do we women—only fair, right?

"In assembly on Wednesday, they introduced you to Zee, Zer and a dozen other pronouns. Is anyone here confused?"

All hands went up. "Yeah, me too. The idea is to not offend anyone who identifies with another gender, but I think it does more to attract attention to the change. I don't believe

163

there is anyone in *this* class who wants to change their boy-girl status, but if that came up, it is not up to you and me to challenge their decision. Hopefully their decision would have involved their parents." She pointed to a boy who raised his hand.

"So, are we keeping 'his' and 'hers'?"

"In my class yes, but if someone changes, it's like Zoe Ann says: none of our business. I want everyone to be respectful. Uh, yes?" She pointed to a girl with her hand raised.

"My daddy says we should pray for trans people. Is that okay?"

That got a huge smile. "Betty, you should *always* listen to your parents first, and I agree with him, but don't say to such a person: 'I'm praying for you' as though you have judged them. Always be considerate and respectful."

Miss Walsh began to stroll down the aisles among her students. "All right then, your homework was to read The Declaration of Independence. What is the meaning of 'all men are created equal and endowed by their Creator with certain unalienable rights'?" She pointed at a boy in the front row.

"Men rule!" Laughter.

She shook her head at him. "Certainly not. All literature uses the terms men and mankind to refer to all humans. Who's this 'Creator', the government?" She ignored Zoe Ann's waving hand and pointed to a girl on the end of the front row. "Suzie?"

"Uh, well, the government makes laws that give us rights."

"True, but are these the *unalienable* rights they refer to here? What is the meaning of unalienable?" Zoe Ann's hand waved alone. Teacher gestured to her.

"It means God gave us rights that came with being created human and *no one* can take them away."

Ms. Walsh smiled. "Ah, so true. Now I know *you* know, but who else remembers what those rights are?" She gestured to the class.

A boy called out, "Life, Liberty and the Pursuit of Happiness."

"Yes!" A double fingered point. "We'll talk about life and liberty tomorrow, but don't you think it is amazing that a government would recognize a right to pursue happiness? I think our country is unique in guaranteeing that."

Walsh squatted down in front of a quiet, homely girl who had been sitting with her head down. "Tell me, Amanda, do you think they meant that the boy next to you would be at liberty to call you names and fling spitballs at you if it made him happy?"

Amanda shook her head violently. "Nah-uh!"

"But what should the government do to stop him?"

165

Big pout. "There's laws and we got police."

"Exactly. Our Founders gave us laws starting with the Constitution, and police to enforce them. Our liberty stops when we violate the rights of others. The police might give a warning first, but offenders risk punishment, *especially* if they do it a second time."

The boy winced at the stern look coming from his teacher. Amanda added a stuck-out tongue.

Miss Walsh got up and resumed her stroll among the students. "The Declaration lists the grievances of the Colonies and in the final paragraph they appeal to the 'Supreme Judge of the world' and state they have a 'firm reliance on the protection of divine Providence.' Who can tell us what our founders mean by all that?"

The class was silent. Finally, one boy spoke up. "In Assembly, the Principal said we shouldn't talk about it."

"Ah, yes. This is a subject that causes fear and loathing to some, but to others, joy and peace. In my class everyone is free to talk about *any* subject. Who has the courage to give a name for our Creator and the Supreme Judge."

Zoe Ann's hand waved with an added 'bouncy-bounce.' "That's *God*, Miss Walsh."

"Quite right." Miss Walsh walked to the front and faced the class. "God has been a subject many consider controversial, but our founders relied on God and his Word in designing our

166

Constitution. Kings and dictators are *furious* about our Constitution and the individual freedom it gives our people. I hope out national motto will always be 'In God We Trust.' My youngest brother is in college. Last month he spent a night in jail just for handing out copies of our Constitution on campus."

"Here's something fun, though. Most of you will be here tomorrow night waiting in the gym while the Parent Teachers Meeting goes on. I'm not scheduled for the first half hour, so if you want, we can go up to the roof and see something special. Anyone want to guess what that is?"

A boy calls out, "We get to watch Mrs. Servis take off on her broom?" Raucous laughter.

"Bobby, that's not nice. No, the planet Saturn is high in the sky and an amateur astronomer is bringing his telescope so we can all have a look at her beautiful rings."

Smart-ass Bobby replies, "So, why is a planet a *she*?"

Ms. Walsh put hands on hips. "Cause only women know how to dress in elegant beauty." She chuckled. "Come and see."

Miss Walsh leaned back against her desk. "All right, it is 'Composition Friday.' You have fifteen minutes to be creative. Remember, your ideas will always be respected, and no subject is off limits. You will only be graded on your use of English and creative expression, but after our discussion of the Declaration, I decided to change the subject I was going to assign. This week, our theme will be why I believe or don't believe in God."

THE EVIL FUTURE?

The Lord abhors the bloodthirsty
And deceitful man. Psalm 5: 6, NKJV

CCP Military Headquarters, August, 2024

General Wang Tsung: "Understand that this briefing will remain confidential with every general and admiral here, and will not be discussed with your staff until the proper time." Heads nodded. "The Chairman has decreed that the reunification of Taiwan will take place in one month." Applause and cheers.

"This is why our troops have been massing at port cities and naval ships have been moved from the south. We will take the island in one massive attack. I will hand out your orders at the end of this meeting but there will be no phone or electronic communication regarding these plans. Understood?"

Tsung pointed to a raised hand, a general sporting a look of concern. "But, Sir, the Americans have pledged to come in defense of Taiwan."

"Oh, yes." Tsung bore a thin smile. "There are two reasons why this will not happen. First, they know we can completely defeat them. They know our surveillance has mapped out every military installation they have, and our navy is far superior now that they have cut their number of ships. Also, many are deployed in the Middle East now. Our cyber units will confound their computers and we can fly supersonic missiles with EMPs to extinguish their electric grids and put the entire USA in the dark. Ground units are now in training to disable any remaining power plants with rifles. With no fuel or electricity for months, the USA would surrender on their knees."

An Admiral said through his laughter, "Who needs a second reason."

Tsung grinned back at him. "But, the second reason is even better. The American president requested it."

He contemplated the silence and the open mouths facing him. "Their president knows Taiwan is going to be ours anyway, but if he can pose as a valiant warrior leader, he hopes to stay in power. Just as we saved him with our virus four years ago, we'll save him again—all to our great benefit as well."

"By letting him attack us?"

"No, no, their response will be just theatrics. We have four ships ready for the scrap heap. They will be towed out and their navy will sink them. We'll even film it for their TV."

"The US agrees to this?"

"Of course. Political victory is everything. When our conquest is complete, their 'heroic' president will broker an end to the war where we promise not to bomb South Korea."

MEDIA MATTERS

You shall not bear false witness against
Your neighbor. Exodus, 20: 16

Owen headed for home after work in Chicago sporting one of the new EMT summer uniforms they had just handed out—tan and brown in light, breathable polyester. His thoughts reviewed his last call--a heart attack due to arrythmia. With the doctor on the phone, they gave the man a drug by IV while enroute. By the time they got to the hospital their patient was sitting up and thanking them. Good thoughts.

Stopped at a traffic light, Owen saw a half dozen black men running toward him from the side street. They stopped as one fell on the sidewalk. Another man stood, staggering by the curb. He pulled over, took out his phone, called 911 for an ambulance and ran toward the man as he was falling, but he slipped on something in the gutter. Both fell on the curb, Owen cradling his head under his arm. Other men shouted at him.

He looked into vacant eyes. "What's going on?" No response. The man was gasping for breath. There were some white pills on the sidewalk and a boy came close and started to pick them up. "Don't touch those, son!"

The man had stopped breathing. No pulse. Owen began chest compressions and rescue breathing.

A police car pulled up, lights flashing. Two men ran away but others pointed at Owen and shouted: "Arrest him. Arrest him. He killed him!"

Two officers rushed toward Owen. One quickly handcuffed him and said to the other, "Check and see if the other guy over there is alive."

Owen pleaded, "I'm a paramedic—just got here. I called 911 for an ambulance."

"No, we did. These guys are shouting that you attacked him."

"Nonsense! I've been trying to save him but I think he OD'd on something, maybe Fentanyl."

Slipping Owen's wrists into handcuffs behind his back, the officer said, "You may be right but we'll sort this out at the station."

The second officer said, "This one's dead, too. I'll get some statements from these witnesses."

With sirens screaming and lights flashing, a second patrol car pulled up. After a brief conversation, Owen was moved to the back seat. "Hey, why don't I drive my car there and give you a rundown." He pointed to his car by nodding his head toward it.

The cop said, "That car? The one parked illegally by the hydrant? Give me your keys. We'll have it towed."

Given his one phone call at the station, Owen told Beth what had happened—clearly a misunderstanding. She'd come with a lawyer in the morning.

*   *   *

NEWS BOX REPORT AT SIX: The reporter spoke opposite a split screen showing two men lying on the street and police cars with flashing lights. "Breaking news. Immediately after a drug bust on Sixth and Vine, two men collapsed after running from the scene, later pronounced dead. Names withheld pending informing next of kin. This video is from the Traffic Cam."

The picture switched to an earlier scene showing one man lying on the sidewalk and Owen rushing to the second man as he

collapsed. "This appears to be a paramedic breaking the man's fall and applying CPR."

The scene switches to the reporter at a desk with another man beside him. "We are fortunate to have with us Mister Derek Sloane, retired Joliet Police Chief. Chief, thank you for being with us. I realize this only happened hours ago, but what do you make of the situation?"

"Thanks for having me. This was apparently a sting operation where officers approached several drug dealers and they attempted to flee. It is common practice for dealers to swallow their drugs so they will have nothing on them when searched."

"Isn't that dangerous?"

"Three or four pills of opioids or Xanax will take fifteen minutes for an effect and the dealer will try to find his car or somewhere to sleep it off after they release him."

"So, you think these two might have gulped their pills— but they're dead, Chief. Do you think they took too many?"

"Sadly, things have changed recently. China has been shipping huge quantities of Fentanyl to be made into tablets in Mexico. Many are deceptively labeled as Xanax or other drugs and even one tablet can deliver a fatal dose. It's poison, really."

"But, Chief, there won't be any returning customers."

"Right. In my opinion it's a Chinese war against American youth—the very men and women who might put on a military uniform."

"That's horrible. Thank you, Chief, for your insight." The camera switches back to the reporter. "We'll await the autopsy report and keep following this story for you. When we come back: an update on parents versus school boards."

*   *   *

BNN TV NEWS AT ELEVEN: The anchor man faced the camera with deep concern. "This just in. Earlier today, two black men have been killed in an apparent hate crime." The video showed a protest at police headquarters with placards and cries for vengeance. "Justice for James Ford, they shouted. Justice, now!"

Anchor man said, "We obtained a video taken from a Traffic Cam." The viewers saw a short clip beginning with Owen colliding with the man, then two seconds of him pounding on his chest. It ended before the rescue breathing began. "I have with me Oliver Spingrift, formerly with the District Attorney's office. Mister Spingrift, what is your assessment of this tragic event?"

Closeup shot of a black, scowling man shaking his head. "While it is too early to reach any conclusion here, it would certainly seem to be a hate crime. Notice how the suspect smashed Mister Ford's head on the edge of the curb--likely the death blow, but still, the killer kept punching the victim."

"I see, but what could be the motive for this violence?"

"If you are in certain supremacist organizations, that is motive enough to commit hate crimes against blacks. I prosecuted many of those when I was in the DA's office."

"Organizations? Can you clarify that for us, Mister Spingrift? They have yet to investigate this killer's background."

"The clue in this case is the khaki pants. They are a subtle marker--a dog whistle if you will, for white supremacy. Remember Hitler's Youth Corps?"

Anchorman nods with a sly grin toward his audience. "Ah, yes. Well, we will follow this story and give you more information as it becomes available."

Before fading to the commercial break, the viewers were treated to fifteen more seconds of angry protestors.

*　　　　　*　　　　　*

Isaiah entered his apartment and called out, "Hi, honey, the Giant Slayer is back." No response. He heard the TV going in the next room. Patti shouted "Bam!"

His wife sat on the edge of the couch intently watching TV with a "stick thing" in her hand. He went over and gave her a cheek kiss. "You heard about my dad being arrested, right?"

"Yeah. I hope Kristin gets him a million bucks for false arrest and defamation."

"Maybe, but they seem to be making a political thing out of it. What's that thing in your hand?"

She ignored the question. "Can you believe my cousin Monica cancelled me? Last month she said I'd fallen off the right side of the boat. Since then, she won't even answer my texts and even our mutual friends aren't speaking to me."

"Bummer. You got cancelled. I call it 'social terrorism,' and it's getting to be their standard way of avoiding intelligent discussions. Are you planning to beat them with that stick?"

Patti chuckled and waved it over her head. It had a light on the tip and she flashed it on and off. "This is Harry Potter's wand. I converted it to a *cancellation* wand and I'm zapping TV people who have it coming. Very satisfying. Want to try it?"

Isaiah took the wand with a sinister, "Heh, heh." He snuggled in next to his wife and was rewarded with a neck tickle. She rewound the program to BNN's report on Owen.

After watching for a minute, Isaiah pointed the wand, flashed the tip and shouted, "Bam! I just cancelled Spingrift."

"Feel better, honey?"

"Much."

BYTE ME

The electronic convention in San Francisco bustled with activity and Isaiah and Patti were enjoying a large reception in the hotel ballroom. She came up behind her husband as he was talking to someone. Her hand touched his shoulder. "Darling, did you know there is a blue bowl over there overflowing with Ghirardelli mints?"

He returned a smile, slipped his arm around her waist and faced the woman he'd been talking to. "Susan March, this is my minty-mouthed wife, Patti."

The woman was dressed in a tweed sports jacket and men's cordovan shoes. Her black hair was tied in a tight bun and her look was austere, but she chuckled and extended her hand. "Nice to meet you. Your husband's work in cyber security programming is widely known in our industry."

"Likewise. He's also the nicest genius you'll ever meet."

"Maybe, but I'm concerned about his taste in wine."

Isaiah held up his cup. "What, it's not bad."

Susan chuckled. "They don't serve the good stuff in plastic glasses. Come over to our table. There's someone I'd like you to meet—and we have a bottle of vintage French

Cabernet." She grinned at Patti. "My wife grabbed a stash of those chocolates you like. Come and save her from eating too many."

She motioned for them to follow and turned away. Isaiah whispered to Patti, "HR exec at Intel."

"Uh, wife?"

He wiggled her shoulder. "Shush."

Intel had reserved three tall round tables with stools. They were directed to one where a man, and one probable man, sat with a woman. Susan looked at Patti then gestured toward the woman. "Guys, this is my wife, Rachel. Staci and Derek, this is Patti and Isaiah. They're a cute cisgender couple. aren't they?"

The men, who wore similar Hawaiian shirts, greeted them. Derek had sandy hair with nice waves, and delicate but sharp features—quite handsome. Stacie sported dangle earrings, long eyelashes, a hint of lipstick and a four-o-clock shadow-- maybe we better switch to the "she" pronoun.

Rachel, a pretty, mid-twenties woman, tossed her wavy auburn hair to one side and pushed two Ghirardellis toward Patti as she sat down beside her. "Here, help me out before my teenage acne returns. Oh, and we're not married yet. Susan just thinks that avoids confusion."

Susan took Isaiah's little cup, poured it out in a tasting bowl and filled it from a bottle. "I think you'll find this a tad better." Gesturing across the table she said, "Derek is doing work in cyber security for us. You two should have a chat later, but not right now. The way you cyber guys talk makes my head hurt."

Derek finger pointed. "Yeah, we've heard about the new program you're working on. Maybe we can lure you to Intel."

Isaiah nodded and complimented the wine. "Let me confess. We were both raised in small town USA, so I hope no one is offended if we get a pronoun wrong."

Susan waved him off. "Don't worry about it. That's something we're all used to, right?" They laughed.

Stacie said, "Okay, but lets clear the confusion for you. I'm Trans—still working on getting the hormones fixed. I won't bother you with the new pronouns so, if you remember, you can use she and her for me. My husband, Derek, is gay-bi, and we haven't been married yet either. We'd like to adopt, but those adoption centers make it difficult for couples like us."

Derek added, "I'm easy—all man." Rachel giggled.

Susan said, "And, Rachel and I are lesbian—well she's bisexual like Derek. We'd like to adopt too. Maybe it'll be easier if we get official marriage papers."

Patti bubbled, "Oh that's so great you all want to raise children. Izzy and I plan to get to that next year when I finish one more degree. Are you all with the same company?"

Stacie swung her finger around. "They all are, but not me. Derek and Rachel are in the same department at Intel."

Isaiah opened his hand toward Rachel. "So, you design cyber programs, too?"

Rachel chuckled. "Goodness, no. I don't even remember my multiplication tables. Derek is the smart one." She gave him a sweet smile. "I do marketing analysis and design ads for what they come up with. We either have to sell his programs or integrate them into what we already have."

Patti pointed at her. "But without your job, the company would go broke."

While they chuckled, Rachel added, "And *one* of those programs," pointing at Derek, "was a pig that got my lipstick."

Derek guffawed. "True, but I worked on it some and added red sneakers and a mustache to piggy before he went out."

For the next half hour, the group made the bottle of Cabernet and the chocolates disappear. The cyber experts talked about the Chinese, the North Koreans and the Russians and their conversations drifted from nanobots to block chains, from cyber defense to national security. Patti and Rachel talked woman talk including more than a few belly laughs.

"Hey!" Isaiah pointed an index finger at the ceiling. "It *just* occurred to me. I have a suggestion to solve all your adoption worries." Two finger points. "Why not have Derek and

182

Rachel here be the ones to marry? A couple of Caribbean Cruises from now and I'll bet you'll all have all the children you want without a single jot of paperwork."

Patti shot up grasping Isaiah by the back of his shirt. "Oh, my gosh. My City Tour is about to leave." A stern look to her husband. "And *you're* supposed to call your boss this afternoon."

Standing and nodding, Isaiah addressed his stunned audience. "Oh, right. Look, I've enjoyed meeting all of you and I'll see you around the convention."

The two quick-stepped out of the meeting hall, and once outside, Isaiah protested: "First, ouch. Let go of my back. Second, Was that such a bad idea?"

Patti headed him out to a vacant outdoor patio. "Sorry if I was rough, dear. My intuition told me that in about ten seconds they would all realize what you just did."

"All right, I guess I was being a lot more spontaneous than Woke. You think they'll be angry?"

Patti laughed. "No, what you did was sheer genius and I like the way you tossed the bomb in with such casual glibness. I just didn't want us to be there when it went off."

"And what does your feminine intuition say about the casualties?"

Patti moved closer and looked around. "Deceptions will die—deceptions of two lovely people concerning same sex relations. Rachel and Derek are in love but in their present circumstances, they're afraid to admit it."

JAIL

Attorney, Kristin Newman, was waiting in the conference room as Owen was led in, hands behind his back, in handcuffs. The guard released him and sat him at a table facing counsel.

When the guard left, Kristin said, "I have to say, you're the last person I expected to see in jail."

"Me too, but this is a simple misunderstanding. I think they'll drop the charges as soon as they understand the truth, don't you think?"

"What should happen and what will happen can be two different things. Do you know that there are protests outside with large photos chanting 'justice for James Ford'?"

"I could hear the chanting, but I couldn't make out the words. Is that the name of the guy who OD'd?"

"Yes, and there are protests in Los Angeles and New York as well. These people organize quickly to put pressure on the District Attorney."

"Good grief! Don't they realize I was trying to save the man's life?"

"They should, and we'll make that case, but these people want to build a racist narrative ignoring any facts that get in the way. The contrast between the TV coverages was dramatic."

Owen slapped his forehead. "It was on *TV*?"

"Yes—National pickup. This makes our case more difficult especially when it comes to the jury selection."

"Oh, great. Next, you're gonna tell me they plan to take me to a firing squad out back. No good news?"

Kristin offered a sympathetic face-squinch. "Sorry, but I have to tell it like it is. Look, they haven't charged you with anything yet, but that should come this afternoon. First, I want you to tell me in full detail what *actually* took place. I will meet with the DA and try demanding that all charges be dropped."

Big sigh. "Okay, you do that. Meanwhile, I'll try and be calm and get back to praying. What are my chances of walking out later?"

"Not good I'm afraid, but we'll find out soon."

CREATIVITY

Miss Walsh entered her classroom with a spring in her step and a twinkle in her eye. "Good afternoon and happy Creative Friday." She dragged her desk chair around to the front and sat facing her students. "I'm impressed with you as a class. In just four months, most all of you have progressed from writing like it was a chore to creating something anyone would enjoy reading. Not only that, a few of you fifth graders are writing at high school level and beyond. Congratulations!"

A boy's hand went up. "Yes, Sean?"

"You're not gonna make us read these aloud like you usually do, are you?"

She shook her head. "No, I promised you'd all be ghostwriters on this assignment. God is a sensitive subject for some, so everyone will remain anonymous. However, the very fact that controversy exists, makes it a good challenge for writers to think about what and how to express themselves."

Miss Walsh was carrying a folder. She crossed her legs and opened it up. "Here's what I'll do today. Without naming the author, I'm going to read a few lines from some of your papers. Just as we need freedom of speech, we all need to be exposed to other points of view."

She smiled at her students. "Some of you look nervous. That's okay. Listening to opinions you don't share is a good thing. The challenge should make you rethink your own ideas rather than being offended. Okay, here goes."

- "I don't see God anywhere, so I won't believe he's real until I see him."
- "I can sense His presence everywhere because there are so many plants, animals and pretty places, all this couldn't be an accident."
- "My parents make me go to church. There are a priest and people in there doing things over and over. If I have to do good all the time, I'm going to hell."
- "My parents love God like they know him. One night I prayed and asked God if He was really there, to show me. I heard Him say He was with me and He loved me."
- "My dad says you can't talk about God in Public School and he's going to report you to the principal."
- Last summer I went to Bible Camp. They prayed and put their hands on me. Then, I knew Jesus was real and inside of me. It really happened.
- This huge earth is but a tiny blue pearl, the great solar system but a little pinwheel, the enormous galaxy just a whirl of water in a brook, and our vast universe with

billions of galaxies merely flickers of light in the hands of our loving God.

"Oh, my." She put a hand to her cheek. "How about that. All right, class, I'm going to stop there. It's no secret that I love creative writing. When you write, you form ideas more clearly in your head, and when you read with an open mind, it's like entering another consciousness." Pointing to a girl's raised hand: "Yes, Zoe Ann?"

"The last one gave me a picture in my head and I want to paint it."

"Perfect. That's what an author strives for. His head picture to yours." Pointing again. "Stephen, go."

"So, it's 'My mind to your mind,' like a Vulcan mind meld." The class laughed.

"Star Trek reruns still playing, huh? All right, time to learn more about sentence structure—not as interesting perhaps, but most important in order to make your writing better. Susan, yes?"

"Will you post those on the bulletin board like you did before?"

"No, they're anonymous. If I do, it will start everyone guessing. However, I will ask the last writer if we can anonymously put his, uh or her, work in the school newspaper."

Now at the blackboard: "Alright, on to sentence diagrams, but write this down. Your weekend creative writing homework theme is, Two Birds on a Branch: 100 words."

DEPRESSION

Emma waited for Patti to arrive at the Daily Grind Coffee Shop and stood up when she arrived. "Thanks for coming. I hope you don't mind but I have a problem to lay on you."

"Not at all, Emma. You are doing such a super job for the campaign. Everyone loves your poster." A waitress appeared at her side. She looked up with a grin. "Sumatra black, and some scones for me, please."

Emma asked for the same and put her hand on Patti's. "First, I want to say how sorry I was to see your father-in-law being arrested. It's so *obviously* political theater. I think they were planning to have riots and expecting his release."

"They're rioting anyway." Patti gave her a grateful look and a head nod. "I appreciate your concern. Our guess is the neo-Marxists had to have something to distract everyone from thinking about rampant inflation, millions of foreigners flooding in, not to mention giving up driving and eating meat. But, hey, what's on your mind?"

"Did you ever meet my friend, Louise Brent?"

"Biker Loulou? Of course. Who could miss her big, noisy arrival at all our college meetings? Too bad about her boyfriend and his accident, though. What's his name?"

"Brad. He lost his left leg below the knee last year, but he's recovered now--walking pretty well with an appliance."

"Praise the Lord."

"Yes, he could have been killed, but what has Loulou going crazy, is his depression. The accident was his fault and he's terribly ashamed of his artificial limb—hasn't been back to work yet and he believes all his former friends think he's a loser. He even thinks Loulou's love is pity. That's a *total* delusion, of course, and he's talked about suicide."

"Does he know Jesus?"

"He does, but he hasn't been to church since the accident and has been avoiding his old biker buddies. Brad lives with his dad whose only message to him has been 'serves you right.' Get the idea?"

"Yeah, he feels guilty and unloved, but what can I do?"

"I dunno, but I thought we could brainstorm about it." Patti nodded, leaned back and sipped her strong coffee. Emma added, "If he would just get back on a bike again, I *know* his friends would give him a hero's welcome."

Patti sat for a while, lids blinking under a wrinkled brow. Suddenly, her pretty eyes flashed wide open. "I have an idea—a weird one, but I think it could be a breakthrough for him."

"How weird?"

She giggled. "A fifth grade one."

*   *   *

Loulou rode up on her boyfriend's motorcycle with a reluctant Brad on the seat behind her. The story they told him was that Zoe Ann always wanted a motorcycle ride, and was all upset about her dad being in jail—all true, but Patti had worked on a surprise for him.

They were greeted with a hug from Beth, and an excited Zoe Ann who ran out to fawn over the motorcycle. Back inside, they all went to Zoe Ann's studio room where Brad told some cycle stories and admired her artwork. At Louise's insistence, Brad wore his motorcycle cut and it was clear that he was warmed by Zoe Ann's adoration. She said his artificial limb was "so cool" and he even let her examine it.

He confessed that he was embarrassed by the metal leg and, true to their master plan, Zoe Ann said, "I know *just* the thing to make you feel better."

For the first time in a year, Brad chuckled. "And what would *that* be, little one?"

Out came the master weapon of little girls—the happy grin of enthusiasm. "I'm gonna draw you such a *super* tattoo on the other leg, no one will even notice."

Brad returned a hearty laugh. "You don't even know *how* to tattoo, little darlin."

"Do too. It'll be a temporary ink one—one that *looks* real, but, if you don't like it, it'll be gone in a month."

Brad leaned forward, closer to her. "And just what do you think you're gonna paint on me?"

Another big grin, "A surprise, but you'll like it. I'll start with your bike logo on top."

Louise knelt beside Zoe Ann. "Better shave this leg first." She pointed at Patti standing nearby, and she rushed off to get the razor. "Brad, slip off your cut so she can see the logo."

Patti came back with a bowl and a razor. "You'll have to be still for a while. Care for some chocolate chip cookies?"

"Ever met a man who said no?" He handed his motorcycle cut to Louise, and removed three cookies from the plate Beth was holding. "You ladies are spoiling me—love it."

Soon, Zoe Ann began work on Brad's leg with furrowed brow. Her tongue poked out the side of her mouth as the biker logo took shape below his knee. The moto: "Ride on King Jesus."

Beth produced a mirror to show mister mouth-full-of-cookies. "Wow, that's awesome, Zoey!"

Zoe Ann moved to his calf. "Now comes the fun part."

Brad asked if she would tell him. "Nope." He chuckled.

193

The ink pen started with two swirling circles. "Those tickle," he said. Zoe Ann giggled. The women scrunched down to see what was emerging—a motorcycle, of course. Brad was riding, and behind him, Loulou waved to onlookers.

"Not done, yet," said the artist as she positioned herself by the inside of his leg. Shortly the cycle was being chased by a tan Golden Retriever.

Louise chuckled. "Who told you about my dog?"

She pointed to Patti. "She did. Now, Brad has to stay here for fifteen minutes in front of a fan to let the ink dry."

Louise put a hand on Zoe Ann's shoulder. "This is absolutely fabulous. While Mister cookie-face has to sit here, I think you've earned a motorcycle ride around the park."

"Gee, *really*?" She looked at Mom who gave a thumbs up, then ran for her jacket. "Quick, before she thinks about it."

When they left, Brad grinned at Beth. Zoe Ann's amazing. Where the heck did you find that kid?"

"Uh, in a utility closet."

Brad was up and thanking the ladies for their hospitality when Louise and Zoe Ann came back amid a chorus of happy laughter. Brad gave Zoe Ann a hug. "Can't thank you enough, little lady. How about I give you a ride to school on Monday?"

That got an up and down jump. "Yea!"

Back out on the street, Louise and Brad waved to the window watchers. Brad climbed up on the seat and took the handlebars and smiled at his girlfriend. "Hop on, Sweetheart. I'll take you home."

MEDIA TRIAL

BNN Evening News: "Andrea Merchant on scene outside the James Ford trial. Closing arguments have just finished and it is now in the hands of the jury. I'm standing in the midst of a large, peaceful protest on behalf of Mister Ford."

She extends her microphone to a black woman with green hair holding a BLM sign. "What do you think the outcome of this trial will be?"

"Oh yeah—slam dunk guilty. If not? Hell to pay. Police attacks on blacks gotta stop."

"But he was an EMT, not police."

"No difference—uniform—city employee—gotta stop."

The reporter faced the camera. "We'll get some more responses and I'll try for the counsel and prosecutor remarks when they leave. Right now, back to you in studio."

A grim-faced anchorman fills the screen. "Thank you, Andrea. While no cameras were allowed in the courtroom, I'm told that the prosecution did a brilliant job in summarizing this atrocious murder for the jury. Next to me is retired Assistant District Attorney Muller from Chicago."

He gestured toward a man wearing a grey pin-striped suit and salty black hair. "Your assessment, sir."

"Thank you for having me. One can never be sure of a jury verdict, but I would be surprised if there wasn't a conviction. The defense kept trying to repeat the idea of a drug dealer bust because there was one nearby. Your viewers are likely unaware that the second man on the pavement was the one who actually *did* die of an overdose. He was White, or I guess Hispanic. Anyway, he was being ministered to by the concerned people around him."

"So, you're expecting a guilty verdict? Why not first-degree murder?"

"The prosecution was wise to indict for second degree. It would be difficult to prove preplanning. I believe the jury will do the right thing."

"Thank you, Counsellor Muller. The jury may reach a verdict as early as tomorrow and we will interrupt our programming for the news as soon as it happens."

NEWS BOX Evening News: The anchorman begins: "Bret Mayer reporting. The Ford trial has just concluded and we'll go to our reporter outside the courthouse, Lisa Combes. They tell me you were injured. Are you okay, Lisa?"

The scene changes to a blonde woman in a crowd with a bright red streak on the side of her forehead. "Lisa Combes here. It's just a cut from something a BLM protester threw at me when I tried to speak with them. Guess they don't like the News Box. Anyway, I'm here with the EMT protesters and their friends who feel Owen Wilson should not have been arrested." She extended her microphone to a man beside her wearing his uniform. "Your feelings, sir."

He moved closer to the camera, his face in distress. "This is an absolute travesty of justice for pure political and evil purposes. I have worked with Owen Wilson. I know him to be a man of fine character, and he's absolutely *not* racist in any way. Look at the whole video. Yes, Owen collided with Ford and they fell, but he was applying CPR, not beating the man."

"In the trial, witnesses claimed he was enraged."

He shook his head. "Enraged? Owen was the one who called 911 before he ran to help. I wish they would have shown a training video of the life-saving chest compressions we use."

"Yes, I suppose that might have had an impression on the jury."

A black female EMT stepped up to the microphone. "I doubt it. The politicians would pass a law that all emergency personnel get retrained in rescue procedures that look better to onlookers."

Lisa asked, "But what about the cause of death? The autopsy report was a heart attack following head trauma."

The woman looked skyward and rolled her eyes. "It makes me both sad and angry to find even the coroners turning political. Yes, there was an abrasion on Ford's face, but *no* cranial bleeding. The big point is, he had a Fentanyl level over twelve. That's *four times* the lethal level and obviously the cause of death."

The male EMT finger-pointed. "The defense made that clear, of course, but prosecution ridiculed them for arguing with a medical professional. We just hope the jury sees the truth of what happened. Oh, and let's dress that forehead wound of yours."

The BLM protesters moved in closer to their interview with a bullhorn, shouting at them. "Racists! White supremacists, go home!"

Lisa dodged a thrown bottle. "I think you get the picture here in front of the courthouse. Back to you in studio, Bret."

From behind his desk, Bret said. "Thank you. Stay safe out there, Lisa."

SCHOOL CHOICE

When you face various trials, know that testing
Of your faith produces patience. James 1:2-3

Celia came in the front door with Zoe Ann. "Hi, Beth, we're home."

Beth hustled over to give her daughter a hug. "Darling, we mustn't be upset by all this. We mustn't believe they are going to send Daddy to jail."

She returned a pout. "Everyone in school says so."

"Well, they'd be sending an innocent man to prison and the verdict's not in yet. I refuse to think the worst." They went to the living room. "Here, sit. Do you want anything to eat?"

Zoe Ann shook her head and slid off her back pack. "Bad day at school, Mom."

Celia said, "The kids were making fun of her. Only Gini stood up for her."

Beth put an arm around her daughter and drew her in close. "Don't mind them. Small minds like to pick on people."

"There's something else real bad, Mom."

"My gosh, darlin. You look so sad. What is it?"

"You remember Johnny Cook, the boy in Junior High who had that surgery to make him into a girl? He jumped off a bridge yesterday—killed himself."

Mother and Celia groaned. She added, "Yeah, and he left a note. They won't tell us what it said, but a girl who knew him said it was just one word: 'Deceived'."

Beth shook her head. "Aaah, that's so, *so* awful! At least your school year is almost over and you'll start Christian Academy this fall. Uncle Fred is covering the tuition and offered to pay Gini's, too. Her mom's excited about it."

"More bad stuff, though—well, bad and good."

Beth slapped her head. "Oh, please. Now what?"

"They cancelled Miss Walsh—said it was for teaching religion."

Celia chirped. "No! She's the best teacher they have."

Zoe Ann held up a finger and grinned. "But, the *good* news is that Christian Academy hired her for sixth grade—right where I'll be."

Beth smiled and gave her a squeeze. "Yea! Sounds like a Holy Spirit thing. Let's put all that bad news behind us."

"I got one more nasty thing to put back there."

Celia gave her cross eyes, but Zoe Ann continued. "Today there was another boy who says he's a girl. He was in our showers playing with his boy thing."

Beth slapped her forehead and stood up. "Okay, maybe you should take sick days for your last week. Look, I have to go for a few hours to cover for someone at work. You two can put on the TV and see if there's any news about the trial."

JURY VERDICT

The Lord is my light and my salvation.

Whom shall I fear? Psalm 27: 1 NKJV

"Cece, I don't want to watch any more cartoons. I wanna watch the trial if it's on."

Celia Holt sat on the couch next to her charge and gently rubbed her back. "I know, but Zoe Ann, it might be more bad news. After all you've just been through, are you sure?"

"I know everybody says Dad is going to prison, but *we* know he didn't do anything wrong, so maybe it will be good news. Anyway, I want to see him."

Celia sighed and switched the channel. Lisa Combes stood outside the court room door, sporting a neat, flesh colored bandage on her forehead. "We are told the jury has reached a verdict and we can go into the court room as soon as they file in. Earlier, State Police were called in when the jury bus arrived. They had to provide a safe corridor to the back door past a horde of shouting protestors."

Lisa was jostled by the nearby reporters and camera men. "Tensions are high here and BLM promises a quote, 'firestorm' if their idea of justice doesn't happen." She put a hand to her earpiece. "Ah, here comes the jury."

After a moment, the scene changes to the courtroom interior and jurors walking in. Zoe Ann gives a little bounce and points. "Look, there's Daddy. He doesn't look happy."

The jury foreman, a middle-aged black woman, remained standing as the others sat. The judge rapped his gavel and addressed her. "Has the jury reached a verdict?"

"We have, your Honor. On the charge of second-degree manslaughter, we find the defendant guilty. On the charge of third-degree murder, we find the defendant guilty. On the charge of unintentional second-degree murder--guilty."

"No!" cried Celia and Zoe Ann together. They held each other and sobbed. Owen's daughter turned her red eyes to Celia. "Just tell me; will I *ever* see my daddy again?"

"Of course, darlin. There's visiting hours, and, besides, I'm sure there'll be an appeal."

In the News Box studio, various experts discussed the verdict for fifteen minutes before the scene changed to the demonstrators outside and the lawyers exiting. Lisa was among others holding out microphones, first to the prosecutor. Another reporter asked, "Are you happy with the verdict, sir?"

"Yes, justice was served and a message has been sent to others who are supposed to serve without racial bias."

The reporters charged over to the exiting defense attorneys and another one got to stick out his mike first. "Ms. Newman, you are the lead defense counsellor. I'm sure you are disappointed with the verdict, but did you really expect this murderer to go free?"

Kristin levelled her gaze at the BNN camera and spoke with firm deliberation. "Owen Wilson is *not* a murderer. He's an Emergency Medical Technician who did his job trying to save a patient. He is innocent of all charges and we will appeal."

The BNN reporter chuckled. "Well, Counsellor, the jury sure didn't think so."

As Kristin and her co-counsellors began to walk away, Lisa got her microphone in. "Attorney Newman, what will be your basis of appeal to correct this travesty of justice?"

Kristin responded, "This was the most unfair trial I have ever seen. We were deluged with jurors who are activists as is the judge. The jurors were clearly threatened and intimidated, two at their homes. We will file for an appeal to the Illinois Court of Appeals requesting a mistrial with a new trial and venue."

Celia sighed, "Nothing more we can do right now."

Zoe Ann looked at Celia, her face tight with determination. "Not true. I know what we can do, Cece."

"Oh, what, Darlin?"

"We can pray."

THE LETTER

The next day, Zoe Ann worked on a painting in her room. It showed Kristin gesturing toward the jury, her face full of passion. Owen sat resolutely, looking at the judge, but there was an angel hovering above him.

She put her brush down abruptly. Sobs were coming from the living room.

Beth sat crying, one hand clutching a piece of paper, the other over her eyes.

Zoe Ann dashed over and slid in next to her mother and hugged. "Did something happen, Mommy?"

"I'm sorry, Sweetie." She kissed her daughter on top of her head. "I was just reading a letter from your daddy that came in the mail. All kinds of feelings just came over me."

"Can you read it to me?"

"Sure, I…" Beth reached for a tissue, wiped her tears and blew her nose. "Of course. I'll try not to cry again."

She smoothed out the letter on her knee as Zoe Ann snuggled closer. "Here goes. *Hello, family. Beth, I want to say how much I appreciated your visit Thursday. Just to hear your voice, see your dear face and hold your hand lifted up my spirits.*

> *Don't be upset that the judge declined the mistrial. That was expected, but the appeal is still out there. Remember how you kid me about changing my plans a lot and not sticking to my planned schedule? Well, here in prison, I'm on a strict schedule every day—just don't ask me about the food.*

> *Here's some good news. My Captain visited me, too. He said that the EMT board voted to put me on sabbatical for six months. I didn't even know there was such a thing, but at least you'll get my salary for a while. Try and be patient. We won't know about the appeal for a few weeks.*

> *Oh, there is a homeless couple in a blue tent by the park fence. I've been praying with them and giving them a twenty every Saturday. I promised them a Bible. Maybe you could stop by with one. His name is Randy, but I don't remember hers.*

> *One more bit of good news: my celle, Sebastian, came to accept Jesus yesterday. He still cries at night but he assures me they are now tears of joy. I admit to a few tears myself. I just miss you all something awful. Keep me in your prayers.*

> *Love and hugs, Owen.*

Zoe Ann's face was squinched tight as she looked up at her mother. "Mommy?"

"Yes, Darlin?"

"Do you think they will ever let Daddy come home?"

VERITAS

The TV panel show "Truth Seeking Ladies," a successful show on News Box, anchored by Lisa Combes is dedicated to controversial themes and opposing points of view. Today's show began with a closeup of Ms. Combes, her forehead scar now barely showing through her makeup. "Hello, and welcome to another slugfest event. This Saturday we are discussing one of the nations most talked about happenings, the conviction of paramedic, Owen Wilson for the death of James Ford."

The camera switches to a wider shot of Lisa flanked by two people sitting on each side of her. "First, on my right, we have two attorneys who were involved in the case." She gestures to a black woman wearing a men's gray suit. "We welcome Maxine Walker from the Southern Protective Law Center who sent briefs in support of the prosecution." Walker frowns silently nodding at the camera.

Lisa gestures to the woman beside her. "Next, we are pleased to have one of the attorneys from the defense team, Kristin Newman from the firm, Schindler, Fitton and Foster."

Kristin smiles. "Thank you, glad to be here."

Lisa returned the smile. "Our pleasure, and on either side are two women who have a personal involvement in the case." The camera pulls in on an attractive, black teenage girl. "This is Moesha Ford, James's younger sister."

She responds with an emotionless, "Hello."

"Finally, we have the daughter in law of the accused, Patricia Wilson."

Her bright face enveloped in curly, blonde hair smiles at the camera. "Thanks for inviting me, Ms. Combes."

"Just 'Lisa' is fine." She faced the camera. "Here are the rules the panelists have agreed to. Each attorney may make an opening statement. We try not to be one of those shows where everyone is interrupting and shouting at one another. As moderator, I will allow for rebuttal, but when a subject area is over, we move on. We'll begin with Maxine."

Maxine's deadpan scowl persisted without a single flicker. "First, I will correct the moderator. We are not discussing the death of James Ford but his deliberate murder at the hands of a white supremacist named Wilson." Patti and Kristin recoiled in disgust, but remained silent.

"The case itself needs no further discussion. This racist bigot was convicted of murder by a jury of his peers and justice has been done. Our organization has identified over six hundred supremacist cells in this country and one of them was only a few blocks away from this vicious attack."

Maxine shook an outraged finger at Kristin. "What we *really* should be discussing is what steps this country needs to take in order to prevent such atrocities, particularly by those who wear government uniforms. I call for mandatory retraining of everyone who dares to ride an ambulance, and the firing of any who are deemed incorrigible."

Lisa broke in. "Maxine, you are getting off topic. Do you have anything more to say about the trial?"

"Sure. The trial gives us a glimmer of hope that justice can emerge if we push back against bigotry and racism. Our democracy is threatened by those who would be the fascist overlords of the minority—by those who would seek to put our people back in chains."

After the stunned silence, Lisa said. "You have one minute more. Anything to say about *the trial?"*

"Yeah. The sentence was too lenient and the protests will continue everywhere until reforms and defunding take place. Viewers can go to the website of Southern Protective Law Center for details." She pushed her chair back and tossed a self-righteous nose skyward.

Lisa turned to Kristin with a pained smile. "I'd guess you would like to respond?"

"About the trial or Maxine's hate-filled neo-Marxist desire to destroy truth, freedom and our American Republic?"

Maxine pointed her finger. "*You're* the ones spreading lies and hate! *You're* the ones who want to enslave the minorities in this country. *You're* the…"

Lisa interrupted. "Rules, *rules*, Maxine. You were not interrupted and Kristin has the floor." Maxine hissed, glowered and looked away.

Kristin smiled at the camera. "All right then, I'll leave the discussion about the violent overthrow of our Country for another time. Owen Wilson's trial, as I have said in previous interviews, was a hugely biased political theater and a travesty of justice."

Maxine stood up, towering over Kristin, pointed again and shouted. "*You're* the travesty of justice. You can't whitewash this, you, you…"

A female security guard moved in next to her and Lisa said, "Maxine, please. You agreed not to interrupt."

"Well, that was before I knew I was to be subject to lying personal accusations and insults to our democracy."

"Please be seated. I'll allow you a minute for rebuttal but Kristin must be allowed to speak."

Maxine was near shouting as she declared, "No, you know what? I've told you what's going down. I'm not gonna listen to this garbage." She threw some papers toward Lisa and stormed out.

Lisa raised her hands and spoke to the audience. "Sorry, folks, that was a first for this show, but we did promise you a slugfest, didn't we? Okay, Kristin, carry on."

"Sure. Getting back to the trial, I believe Maxine has just made one of my points for me. Ideology and ulterior motives overwhelmed any hope for justice. We are appealing in the hope of getting a change of venue for a new and fairer trial."

Lisa said, "But you will have to show specific reasons for a new trial, not just the prevailing atmosphere."

"Of course. Here are the highlights of our appeal. First, we will document that four of the jurors are social justice activists who condemned white individuals in the past. The judge disallowed our intended showing of a CPR video demonstrating that the actions of Mister Wilson were actually *lifesaving*. He also allowed the prosecution to show an edited version of the surveillance recording but would not let us show the full version. That one revealed that both of the deceased were signing they could not breathe before they collapsed."

"But, Kristin, surveillance cameras film long stretches. It would be normal to just show the pertinent footage."

Kristin chuckled. "Traffic cams do not cut off one side of a picture and zoom in. It's laughable that onlookers testified they were trying to help the first guy who fell. Actually, one of them was going through his pockets and removing stuff."

"All right, but I doubt you will get a new trial without specifics about the death."

"Of course. To begin, we were not allowed to cross examine the medical examiner. He was on sabbatical so we were left with his assistant who was not an MD. She basically answered all questions by reciting the written report. It said the cause of death was a heart attack brought on by head trauma and fear. The only head trauma was a cheek abrasion, nothing compared to Mister Wilson's right arm where he cradled his fall. Heck, your forehead gash from BLM was worse. Besides, Mister Ford was twenty-two with no known health problems."

"So, you made the claim that his death was drug related?"

Kirstin sighed and released a breath. "My exact question to her was, 'Don't you think that the 12.2 Fentanyl level, four times the lethal dose, should have been reported as the cause of death?' She only responded that that might have been contributory and was listed on page three."

The camera flashed to Moesha, chin on chest, weakly shaking her head. Lisa said, "Sure looks to me that you have a good case for a retrial. Anything else?"

"Just that the juror bus was met with protests when they arrived at court and three juror's homes, who were not activists, were picketed. Their addresses were doxed. I wish I could be more optimistic but it was leaked that the judge won't give us a new venue. Our only hope may turn out to be praying for a presidential pardon."

"But, you described illegal jury tampering. We have to take a break, but when we come back, we'll talk with the family members affected by Ford's death and the trial. Stay tuned."

VICTIMS

"All right." Lisa turned to Moesha Ford. "Our hearts go out to you, Moesha. We can only imagine the pain of losing your brother so suddenly. Tell us about yourself and anything you'd like to say about James."

"Well, I, uh…" She glanced around at the cameras and the studio.

"Relax, dear. We're all friends here. We'd just like to know more about you and James."

"Okay. I'm almost thirteen and I should be in seventh grade, but I'm starting sixth. My mom died having me—ain't got a father—Jimmy neither. We live with great grandmom but she's goin' ta Medicaid nursing so I don't know what's happening next."

She sat in silence for a moment while the camera went to Kristin, nodding her head and to Patti, her face full of compassion. "Uh, Jimmy was all we had. He paid the rent cause Grammy didn't get enough from security. Yeah, Jimmy sold drugs—stole a few cars, too. He coulda been an auto mechanic but gave it up."

"Was Jimmy ever in jail?"

"A few overnights is all. DA don't prosecute small stuff. Why would anyone make a Xanax pill that's really Fentanyl?"

"That's a very good question, Moesha. That poison has killed a hundred thousand young Americans who were deceived into thinking they were taking something else. So, no long prison time for Jimmy?"

"Nah--like nobody gets time no more. Jimmy said if the cops show up, you just swallow your samples and they got nutin' on you."

"Moesha, do you think that's what happened that night?"

"Oh, yeah. It was near that college. Jimmy said they eat Xanax like candy there—a real gold mine for him. Some pills are supposed to be laced with a *trace* of Fentanyl, but I guess some musta been pure stuff." Her head fell back on her chest and she began to sob.

"We are so, so sorry this happened, Moesha." Lisa put her hand on her shoulder for a few silent moments. She turned to the last panelist. "Patricia is the daughter in law of Owen Wilson. His legal team did not want the immediate family making statements prior to their appeal request. What would you like to say, Patricia?"

"Just call me 'Patti.' Uh, I should say I talked with Moesha in the Green Room and she's a real nice kid who loves

Jesus. Given half a chance she'll do real well." Smiles were exchanged.

"My father-in-law is the nicest man I've ever met—no kidding. He always looked to help others and he's the very *opposite* of prejudice. I hope I don't get him into more trouble, but about twelve years ago he rescued an infant from death at an abortion mill. Not only that, he and his wife adopted the infant, and now, Zoe Ann is the most brilliant, fun teenager—like *ever.*"

Moesha waved her hand. "Uh, can I say something I forgot?" Lisa gestured, sure.

"Maxine told me I'm just supposed to say I was a victim too, and keep quiet, but I hafta say something." She turned to Patti. "I know your dad didn't kill my brother."

Everyone froze. In the silence, a wide-eyed Kristin made the "Cha-ching" motion.

With a voice choked with emotion, Patti said, "Oh, darlin, that means *so* much to me and our whole family. Thank you."

Tears streamed down Moesha's cheeks. "Well, it's *true,* and I ain't no victim neither. They're sending me to foster care. Maybe that's best. I'll just figure out how to manage."

Patti plunked both hands down on the table. "Say, maybe you won't have to figure out *everything* on your own. I

218

know a mom who's raising a kid whose mother died too. Zoe Ann's about your age and her BFF is a black girl named Gini."

Patti's hand found Moesha's and they faced each other. Lisa whispered into her mike, "Forget my closing monologue."

Moesha said. "How old is Zoe Ann?"

"Twelve and going into sixth grade like you. You two need to meet, and if her mom can't adopt you, Izzy and I will so you guys can still hang out and go to school together."

Patti stood up and Moesha scooted over and embraced her. Patti croaked, "We've got Jesus, you know. With Him on our side, there's *nothing* we can't do."

Camera shots of Lisa and Kristin with happy grins on their faces.

Moesha held Patti out at arm's length. "Maybe it's just like Gramma told me."

"What's that, darlin?"

"She said in Isaiah it's written that God can bring joy out of our ashes."

THE FUTURE'S FUTURE?

Save yourselves from this corrupt generation. Acts 2:40, NIV

THE WHITE HOUSE, JULY 4, 2028

A newly formed special forces unit guarded the ballroom and no reporters were present. Lucious Warlock, the recently installed President of the United States, strode to the dais to address a gathering of sixteen elite billionaires from around the globe. He received their applause with a nod and a thin smile.

"First of all, I will thank all of you for entrusting me with this office. I will not let you down." More applause. "Our Progressive Road and our transition to The New World Order may have had some bumps along the way, but we should pride ourselves that complete control is now within our grasp."

"Looking back, let us admit that the forces clinging to their God, and the cancer that was 1776, are not dying easily. They surprised us in 2016, but we thought we had things under control by 2024." Warlock put his hand on his forehead. "Ugg, what a calamity, yes? Our swing state voting system stood ready to handle even a ten-point loss, but the enemy produced twelve. And that was despite a hundred inditements against theirs, and our man being hailed as a war hero in defense of the losing battle for Taiwan."

"Before we could get rid of *that* President—I won't even mention the name—our political prisoners from January 6th and that racist murderer, Owen Wilson, had been pardoned."

"At the midterm, with your billions, and our improved voting system, we regained congress and impeached both the President and Vice President to install our house speaker." Big grin. "From that point on, we quickly added two new states, four more senators and six judges to the Supreme Court. This allowed us to rewrite those awful parts in the Constitution and ensure that our power will never be taken away again." Applause.

"So, where do we go from here? I am grateful that two of you have arranged to buy The News Box." He pointed to two smiling men lifting up their brandy glasses. More applause. "Our administration will not disappoint you. Soon, all education will be under State control, and we are poised to use emergency powers and nationalize all energy. Only then will we gradually reveal the truth about our climate hoax and resume using fossil fuels." The audience rapped on their tables and cheered.

"Oh, before you ask, we are closing in on rebels from those house-church meetings. Their Bible is really a political instrument, you know. Most denominations have submitted to our ideology now so, like China, we will assume all the

Christian churches into our State Church and our rewritten Bible. Questions?"

An elderly man shook his head. "The Catholics will never agree."

"Oh, right," he chuckled. "We won't bother them since they're already complicit, but later we'll be selecting their new Bishops and Cardinals." He finger-pointed at a raised hand.

"My sources tell me the Conservatives are organizing a revolt in their world-wide house churches and other meetings."

"Well, of course they are, and they expect their God to protect them, don't they?" Laughter. "Look, everyone is under surveillance. Between cell phone locators, the internet and face recognition technology, our CIA computers know everyone's movements, and what they say and do. We have established a Police State and converted all wealth to digital currency. As you know, owning gold is illegal once more—without a permit, of course." Laughter.

"Cash and gold was confiscated from safe deposit boxes and we know where most of the guns are. As soon as we root out bad apples from our military, all civilian guns will be confiscated house by house. There will be no revolution."

Another raised his hand. "But, establishing a State Church and disarming citizens is specifically prohibited by the constitution."

Warlock tilted his head and returned a condescending smile. "Sir, those are just words. We control the meaning of words." He straightened up and spread out his hands to the gathering. "The remaining true Christians and Conservatives are communicating with each other by texting. About ninety million receive Bible quotes weekly and a call to prayer. We suspect an imbedded code system—extra spaces and added commas for example. We have cryptographers at work to break it."

Warlock pointed to another man who raised his hand. He said, "Yeah? Why not confiscate the phones, and what kind of quotes are going around?"

"For now, we want them to keep their phones. We track their locations and we are working to locate their leader. The code word they gave him is 'Savior J.' Some think he'll make his big move in 2030, but when he's captured, we will have a public execution."

A man with a heavy German accent spoke out. "Just recently you told us you were closing in. What happened?"

Worlock sighed. "One group texted that 'Savior J is with us now.' When we got there, all we found were seven smiling ladies at a nursing home in New Jersey. He must have escaped."

"What about the quotes?" came the shout.

"Again, I said the quotes themselves are not important—just the messages they are hiding in the words."

An audience shout out: "Humor us. Give an example."

He blew out an impatient breath and fumbled through a folder on the podium. "Okay, the one going out last week was: 'Wickedness will not deliver those who are given to it.' This week, uh…" He turned to one side. "Charon, do you have a copy of what just came in?"

A woman in a navy-blue pants suit hastened up to him, and handed him a phone. "Two quotes today, Sir."

Right," he said, squinting at the message. "This week's reads, 'Evil men and imposters will grow worse and worse, deceiving and being deceived, but the Holy Scriptures are able to make you wise for salvation through faith in Christ Jesus.'" His face contorted in horror at the next line. He gagged, his elbows crashing down on the podium as he flung back her phone and croaked, "Enough!"

Charon thought she was being asked to read the final message and called it out to all the people: "Any man not found in the Book of Life will be cast into the Lake of Fire." *

*The quotes were excerpted from Ecclesiastes 8:8, 2Timothy 3:12-14 and Revelation 20:15.

Pascal John Imperato began writing fiction in Junior High, became a literary editor in High School, and wrote short stories in Creative Writing classes at Johns Hopkins University. Getting a Medical Degree at Duke University, and beginning a medical practice in Pennsylvania temporarily resulted in scientific and journal writing.

After a born-again revelation, he resumed writing fiction, but with a messianic twist under the pen name, "John Pascal." He has published Sci-Fi, "The Revelation Trilogy" novels: "The Bee," "Domes," and "2248." Next, he authored a two book angel series: "Wingin' It," and "My Child" featuring the disabled, and unwanted pregnancy respectively. "Prisoner 1171" followed, a novel focusing on evangelism in prison, and a novella, "Fatherless," dealing with street gangs and human trafficking. After that, he released "Adrift," showing Christian rescues of the homeless. Finally, "Truth Wars," met the challenge of disinformation, censorship and propaganda that is trying to replace truth in our schools. All are Christian friendly.

These books are available on Amazon and Kindle. Further details on Amazon and at "JOHNPASCAL.com."

www.ingramcontent.com/pod-product-compliance
Lightning Source LLC
Chambersburg PA
CBHW022046240626
47154CB00007B/2580